At Issue

| Public Outrage
| and Protest

Other Books in the At Issue Series

At Issue

Public Outrage and Protest

Eamon Doyle, Book Editor

GREENHAVEN
PUBLISHING

Published in 2020 by Greenhaven Publishing, LLC
353 3rd Avenue, Suite 255, New York, NY 10010

Articles in Greenhaven Publishing anthologies are often edited for length to meet page
requirements. In addition, original titles of these works are changed to clearly present
the main thesis and to explicitly indicate the author's opinion. Every effort is made to
ensure that Greenhaven Publishing accurately reflects the original intent of the authors.
Every effort has been made to trace the owners of the copyrighted material.

Cover image: Joshua Lott/Getty Images

Library of Congress Cataloging in Publication Data

Names: Doyle, Eamon, 1988–editor.
Title: Public outrage and protest / Eamon Doyle, book editor.
Description: First edition. | New York : Greenhaven Publishing, 2020. |
  Series: At issue | Includes bibliographical references and index. |
  Audience: Grade 9 to 12.
Identifiers: LCCN 2018058990| ISBN 9781534505278 (library bound) | ISBN
  9781534505285 (pbk.)
Subjects: LCSH: Political violence—United States—Juvenile literature. |
  Protest movements—United States—Juvenile literature. | Political
  culture—United States—Juvenile literature.
Classification: LCC HN90.V5 P83 2020 | DDC 303.6—dc23
LC record available at https://lccn.loc.gov/2018058990

Manufactured in the United States of America

Website: http://greenhavenpublishing.com

Contents

Introduction

O ne of the many unique features of democratic society is the presence of legitimate protest and public political dissent. In the context of traditional or authoritarian forms of government, such behavior is typically forbidden (either by law or edict) and likely to be met with repressive force. But in a democracy, citizens are theoretically free to express dissent and opposition to elected officials and the agencies of government, and to do so in public without fear of reprisal from law enforcement. The benefits of such an arrangement are largely self-evident; when citizens are able to express themselves freely in addition to the formal power they wield in the electoral process, it will theoretically encourage those in power to pursue policies that promote happiness and well-being as conceived by their constituents.

For its part, the United States has a long tradition of spirited public demonstration, a tradition that has included moments of inspiring positivity as well as of violence and hatred. This reflects one of the basic trade-offs of democratic governance: that freedom (of speech and demonstration) is often disruptive and can easily become dangerous when emotions run high and large numbers of people are involved. In the 1960s, the Vietnam War and the civil rights movement provoked major, large-scale protests across the country, including the riots outside the Democratic National Convention in Chicago in 1968 and the incident at Kent State University in which four student protesters were shot and killed by members the National Guard. For a time, historians would point to the era as a sort of high-water mark of outrage and political unrest in the United States.

But over the last twenty-five years, the political atmosphere in the United States has become increasingly polarized and acrimonious, prompting more frequent and intense expressions of public outrage. Examples of this trend include the "Tea Party" demonstrations in the early years of former President Obama's administration as well as the numerous liberal demonstrations in opposition to President Trump and his policies. It appears in many ways as though we have returned to (or perhaps even surpassed) the level of national angst that Americans lived through in the 1960s.

Changes in the media environment have played a major role in laying the groundwork for this renewed tide of national outrage in the United States. Jeffrey M. Berry and Sarah Sobieraj, both professors at Tufts University who collaborate frequently on research related to modern political sociology, outline the media's role in these changes:

The ascent of outrage says more about changing media technologies and regulatory guidelines and the broader culture than it does about the political views of most citizens. Various changes have coalesced to make scream politics a lucrative, sound business strategy. Media regulation has been reduced, freeing outlets to say almost anything. Cable television multiplies outlets competing to grab eyeballs and ears in their own niches. And political life has become intensely personally focused. Together, these shifts encourage media strategies unimaginable even 20 years ago, when outlets used pleasant and inoffensive content to appeal to the broadest possible audiences. Nowadays, controversial, attention-grabbing content helps to draw an audience in a cluttered media landscape characterized by seemingly limitless options. [1]

The chain of events and social transformation that Berry and Sobieraj describe shows that the way people receive information has a profound impact on the way that they translate that information into political preferences and action. This clearly has major implications for political and policy professionals as they seek to understand voter preferences and the temperature of the electorate in general. But, ultimately, protest and outrage represent something broader and deeper than the events or the tenor of any one historical era or policy issue.

Democracy is built on the concept of *government by consent* and public figures, whose power depends on the results of elections. In the broad history of human civilization, democracy stands out against the backdrop of cruelty and suffering that other forms of government and social organization (tribal societies, feudal systems, dictatorships) have caused. In this context we can see protest as a vehicle for individuals to protect themselves from the vicissitudes of human power structures. Elected officials understand that widespread outrage and public protest are an indication that their position may be in jeopardy. It helps them to understand how policies are affecting their constituents and how their constituents feel about it. In other words, protest is a channel through which citizens can exert influence separately from the normal electoral process in a context from which conflict is unlikely to disappear.

This is partly the result of the fact that we live in a large, diverse, pluralistic society and partly the result of competitive social dynamics that emerge around free market economies. But it also has to do with evolutionary psychology and basic aspects of human nature. In an essay titled "The Age of Outrage," the moral psychologist Jonathan Haidt outlines his theory on the inevitability of social and political angst, a theory he developed in his award-winning and highly controversial book *The Righteous Mind*:

> *When we look back at the ways our ancestors lived, there's no getting around it: we are tribal primates. We are exquisitely designed and adapted by evolution for life in small societies with intense, animistic religion and violent intergroup conflict over territory. We love tribal living so much that we invented sports, fraternities, street gangs, fan clubs, and tattoos. Tribalism is in our hearts and minds. We'll never stamp it out entirely, but we can minimize its effects because we are a behaviorally flexible species.* [2]

Haidt's theory points at the beating heart of the democratic project—to organize political conflict such that diverse groups of people can coexist peacefully and cooperatively, despite deep disagreements in the realm of values and morality. It also indicates how radical, ambitious, and fragile a project it is. *At Issue: Public Outrage and Protest* will present viewpoints that examine the nature of political conflict, evaluate its place in US politics, and discuss if—and how—it might have a place in an effective democracy.

Notes

1. "The Roots and Impact of Outrage-Mongering in U.S. Political-Opinion Media: Research Brief," by Jeffrey M. Berry and Sarah Sobieraj, *Journalist's Resource*, October 28, 2014.

2. "The Age of Outrage," by Jonathan Haidt, Manhattan Institute for Policy Research, Inc., previously published by City Journal, December 17, 2017.

1

Rhetoric and Violence: The Wounding of US Representative Gabrielle Giffords

Corey Dade

Currently the head of global media relations at the Bechtel Corporation, Corey Dade began his career as a correspondent for National Public Radio.

In this viewpoint, Corey Dade explores the relationship between political anger and violence through the lens of the 2011 shooting in Arizona that wounded US Representative Gabrielle Giffords. Hot-button political issues like the immigration debate and the violent rhetoric surrounding these issues can lead to violent and extremist actions like Representative Giffords' shooting, showing the potentially deadly impacts of America's extreme political culture.

The shooting of Rep. Gabrielle Giffords (D-AZ) has raised concerns about the effect of inflammatory language that has become a steady undercurrent in the nation's political culture.

Saturday's shooting spree, which killed US District Judge John M. Roll and five others, followed years of hot political debate in Arizona. Both Roll and Giffords had been the subjects of threats in recent years.

Arizona has become one of the most reliably conservative states, particularly in the debates over immigration and health care—two issues that put Giffords, a moderate Democrat, and Roll at odds with many Arizonans.

Members of Congress and other elected officials say violent threats occasionally come with the job, but many politicians and others assert that the shootings reflect a national political culture that has become too heated and rife with instigation to violence.

Hopefully this gives the nation pause, and we can temper down the vitriol toward politicians," Rep. John Larson (D-CT) told reporters outside his home Saturday night. In a news conference Sunday, Larson said Democratic and Republican lawmakers this week will discuss taking new safety precautions, such as requesting a local police presence when they make official appearances in their districts.

In the Senate last year, the number of significant threats directed at members increased to 49 from 29 in 2009, according to the chamber's sergeant-at-arms.

An April 2010 survey by the Pew Research Center found "a perfect storm of conditions" contributing to Americans' distrust of government, including "a dismal economy, an unhappy public, bitter partisan-based backlash and epic discontent with Congress and elected officials."

Mark Potok of the Southern Poverty Law Center, which tracks extremist groups, says inflammatory political rhetoric has risen as a result of the immigration debate. And more recently, he says, the weak economy and the election of President Obama have led to a 50 percent increase in the number of so-called hate groups.

"Earlier in the decade, it was paramilitary groups and nativists who were reacting to illegal immigration," Potok said. "But then you have the first black president and the economy, which just exacerbates the feeling among some whites that they are losing opportunities, or losing their country.

"Now you're seeing a cross-fertilization between those groups from the early 2000s and the people who are upset over Obama and the economy."

Some lawmakers remain circumspect about drawing such conclusions. Giffords' colleague from Arizona, Republican Rep. Trent Franks, declined to say Sunday whether he believes the shootings were motivated in any part by heightened vitriol in public discourse.

"The central element here is this unhinged lunatic that had no respect for innocent human life [who] was willing to make some grand statement. I don't even know if he understands what statement he was trying to make," Franks said on CNN's *State of the Union*. "There is really the central problem—a lack for respect for human life."

Political Fallout in Congress

Lawmakers in both parties over the weekend avoided speculating about any political fallout from the shooting.

House Majority Leader Eric Cantor (R-VA) decided to suspend legislative activity scheduled for this week, a move that at least temporarily prevents another potential escalation in the debate over the health care law. That issue has led to previous threats against Giffords and stirred much of the vitriol characterizing politics over the past two years.

Repealing the health care law is one of the Republicans' top priorities in the new session. The measure is all but assured of passage in the Republican House and rejection by the Democratic-controlled Senate.

In a news conference Sunday, House Speaker John Boehner (R-OH) said the incident should remind his colleagues that their job "comes with a risk." However, he said, "No act ... must be allowed to stop us from our duty."

Security personnel aren't assigned to House members, and many lawmakers say they likely won't scale back their public appearances. Often, though, large events in House members' districts do include a local police presence.

Protecting lawmakers has become more difficult in the past decade, said William Pickle, a former Senate sergeant-at-arms. Appearing Sunday on CNN's *State of the Union*, he said the availability of information on the Internet can guide would-be plotters—even as demands for lawmakers to make public appearances have increased.

"The very nature of being a public official is one where you have to press the flesh. You want as much exposure as you can possibly have. That's not going to end," Pickle said. "We are going to fall back into being complacent again. I hate to say that, but we will. We do not have the resources to protect 535 congressmen and senators."

Pickle, also a retired Secret Service agent who once oversaw the protection of Vice President Al Gore, added that the threats are "impossible to stop. Until candidates stop campaigning, these things tragically are going to continue happening."

Feeling the Heat in Arizona

Some Arizona politicians from both parties say the incident demonstrates the need to defuse their state's highly charged discourse.

The health care overhaul has been a flashpoint for Giffords' constituents. In August 2009, when opponents of the health care bill held demonstrations across the nation, a protester at one of Giffords' events was removed by police when a pistol he had holstered under his armpit dropped to the floor.

Last March, after the bill passed—with Giffords' support—the windows of her Tucson office were broken or shot out by vandals. Similar acts of vandalism against other members of Congress were also reported, including a controversial allegation that a Tea Party demonstrator spat on an African-American congressman while other demonstrators shouted racial epithets. Tea Party leaders have challenged those claims.

But in Arizona, the most divisive issue has been immigration. Arizona is home to many of the staunchest opponents of citizenship for illegal immigrants. It also has the nation's toughest law aimed at identifying, prosecuting and deporting illegal immigrants.

Pima County Sheriff Clarence Dupnik, a Democrat and friend of Giffords, lambasted his home state on Saturday as "the Mecca for prejudice and bigotry."

"When you look at unbalanced people," Dupnik said, referring to accused shooter Jared Lee Loughner, "how they respond to the vitriol that comes out of certain people's mouths about tearing down the government, the anger, the hatred, the bigotry that goes on in this country is getting to be outrageous."

Last year, Dupnik vowed that his deputies wouldn't enforce the state's new immigration law, calling it "racist" and "unnecessary."

Also last year, Dupnik accused Tea Party activists of bigotry and stifling rational debate on immigration—adding that, "We didn't have a Tea Party until we had a black president."

Arizona Tea Party leaders vehemently denied Dupnik's accusations and noted that they didn't take a public position on the immigration law. On Saturday, local Tea Party leaders released statements expressing condolences to the shooting victims' families. They also sought to distance their groups from any suggestion that Loughner was a Tea Party activist or that his attack was politically motivated.

Giffords narrowly won a third term in November against Jesse Kelly, a Republican backed by the Tea Party. Last June, Kelly held an event promoted with the message: "Get on Target for Victory in November ... Help remove Gabrielle Giffords from office ... Shoot a fully automatic M16 with Jesse Kelly."

"They're jumping to this conclusion that it has to do with [Giffords'] hotly contested Congressional race," Allyson Miller, a founder of Pima County Tea Party Patriots, told the website TalkingPointsMemo. "Well, apparently, from what I've seen so far ... it's looking like that's not the case."

Miller and other Tea Party leaders said they won't change their aggressive tactics in the wake of the shootings.

The Cross Hairs Controversy

During the midterm elections, Giffords and other Democratic House candidates were featured on the website of Sarah Palin's political action committee with cross hairs over their districts. Giffords, disturbed at the reference, said at the time, "When people do that, they have got to realize there's consequences to that."

In a Sunday interview with talk radio host Tammy Bruce, Rebecca Mansour, who works for Palin's PAC, said the images of cross hairs weren't intended to evoke violence: "We never, ever, ever intended it to be gun sights," she said.

The images were removed from the website this weekend.

On Sunday, President Obama ordered flags at federal buildings to be flown at half-staff. He postponed his trip to a General Electric facility in New York scheduled for Tuesday.

He also called on the country to join him Monday at 11 a.m. ET in observing a moment of silence for the shooting victims.

"It will be a time for us to come together as a nation in prayer or reflection, keeping the victims and their families closely at heart," the president said in a statement.

2

The Trauma of Racial Violence

Kenya Downs

Kenya Downs is a producer for PBS Newshour. She specializes in multimedia content centered on social justice issues in the United States.

In this viewpoint, Kenya Downs examines the manner in which media imagery can shape and intensify the emotional impact of news about racism and racial violence. While some assert that showing footage of violence against people of color on the news and social media helps bring attention to racism and police brutality, Downs claims that it can also cause intense psychological and emotional distress to viewers and play into the dehumanization of the marginalized victims. Constant exposure to images of race-based violence can exacerbate the trauma and cause further racial tension.

When video of the Baton Rouge shooting death of Alton Sterling first surfaced on July 5, social media networks became immediately populated with Sterling's final moments. The following day, the shooting death of Philando Castile was streamed live by his girlfriend on Facebook. The video, which shows Castile gasping for air after being shot four times by a Minnesota police officer, has since been shared on Facebook more than 5 million times.

"When Black Death Goes Viral, It Can Trigger PTSD-Like Trauma," by Kenya Downs, NewsHour Productions LLC, July 22, 2016. Reprinted by permission.

Outrage peaked again after cell phone footage captured a North Miami police officer shoot an unarmed caretaker as he lay on the ground with his hands up. Charles Kinsey, a behavioral therapist, was aiding an autistic patient who wandered away from his assisted living facility. Kinsey survived with minor injuries. Now, footage of the fatal shooting of Terence Crutcher in Tulsa, Oklahoma, has people calling for justice yet again. The 40-year-old was shot and killed by Tulsa police officer who responded to a report of a stalled SUV.

Escaping the imagery can be nearly impossible, especially as online users post commentary and news updates. For some, it can merely be a nuisance. But research suggests that for people of color, frequent exposure to the shootings of black people can have long-term mental health effects. According to Monnica Williams, clinical psychologist and director of the Center for Mental Health Disparities at the University of Louisville, graphic videos (which she calls vicarious trauma) combined with lived experiences of racism, can create severe psychological problems reminiscent of post-traumatic stress syndrome.

"There's a heightened sense of fear and anxiety when you feel like you can't trust the people who've been put in charge to keep you safe. Instead, you see them killing people who look like you," she says. "Combined with the everyday instances of racism, like microaggressions and discrimination, that contributes to a sense of alienation and isolation. It's race-based trauma."

While research on the psychological impact of racism has only emerged within the last 15 years, Williams says it's "now starting to get the attention that it deserves" and experts are "seeing very strong, robust and repeated negative impacts of discrimination."

A 2012 study found that black Americans reported experiencing discrimination at significantly higher rates than any other ethnic minority. The study, which surveyed thousands of African-Americans, Hispanics and Asian-Americans, also found that blacks who perceived discrimination the most, were more likely to report symptoms of PTSD. Although African-Americans have a lower risk for many anxiety disorders, the study reported a PTSD prevalence rate of 9.1 percent in blacks, compared to 6.8 percent in whites, 5.9 percent in Hispanics, and 1.8 percent in Asians.

Social media and viral videos can worsen the effects. During the week of Sterling's and Castile's deaths, a scroll through timelines of black social media users could uncover subtle expressions of mental and psychological anguish, from pleas for others not the share these videos, to declarations of a social media hiatus. Williams says that's not unusual. These expressions of anger, sadness and grief can hint at something much more serious.

"It's upsetting and stressful for people of color to see these events unfolding," she says. "It can lead to depression, substance abuse and, in some cases, psychosis. Very often, it can contribute to health problems that are already common among African-Americans such as high blood pressure."

That stress is the reason why April Reign refuses to share the graphic final moments of Alton Sterling and Philando Castile. In a column for the *Washington Post*, the former attorney and now managing editor for *Broadway Black*—which reports on African-Americans in the performing arts—calls the need to share viral footage of police shootings "a sick sort of voyeurism."

"We're witnessing mentally and emotionally traumatizing videos and pictures. It's enough, it's just enough. It's just so overwhelming all the time," she told *The NewsHour*. "There are people who are having trouble sleeping, who are having trouble eating. There are people who are having those symptoms of PTSD in the truest sense."

Reign says opponents have pointed out that it sometimes takes the graphic videos going viral before issues of police brutality and racial bias are given any attention. Both Sterling and Castile's deaths sparked national and international protests after first being shared among black users of platforms like Facebook and Twitter. While Reign agrees, she calls decisions to shield certain footage "selective censorship," often influenced subconsciously by racial bias.

She points to last August as an example, when many national media outlets opted not to air the graphic footage of news reporters in Virginia as they were shot and killed by a former coworker on live television. Many news organizations cited respect for the victims and their families as the basis of their decision. Reign says that sense of humanity isn't typically given to victims of color, especially black-Americans. Instead, their gruesome final movements are replayed again and again for all to see.

"It is a dehumanization of black people, and we don't see that with any other race. It's ingrained in us from our history," she says. "White people used to have picnics at hangings and at lynchings, bringing their children to watch black bodies suffer and die. We are not far removed from that, it's just being played out through technology now. And it hurts."

Dr. Williams says that history of racism, passed down through generations of storytelling, can become crippling when combined with personal experiences, including daily microaggressions—subtle, racially-insensitive comments or acts such as a person of color being followed in a store, or having their name mocked or mispronounced by peers.

The physical impact is something Black Lives Matter activist Brittany Packnett knows all too well. "Racism is not real to a lot of people, period," she says, "But what people also don't seem to get is how [black people] internalize that racism and manifest that suffering because, for so long, we've been conditioned to hide it. But's real. It marks us everyday."

Packnett can recall every time she learned of a new person of color killed by law enforcement. In each instance, she struggled with whether to watch the video, and can recount the emotional reaction when she did.

"I hadn't had nightmares about Ferguson and tear gas or protests for a long time, but they came back when I saw those videos," Packnett says referencing the shootings of Sterling and Castile. Avoiding them wasn't an option. Both, she says, were set to automatically play on her Facebook timeline.

"I saw the Tamir Rice video while sitting in the parking lot next to the park where he was killed. In hindsight, did I need to feel that pain watching the video in order to fully absorb what clearly was a tragedy? No. So why did I? Pressure."

Packnett said that activists also feel an expectation to speak authoritatively on these subjects immediately after. "We're supposed to be able to provide language for people's grief that is informed. And in order for it to be informed, there's this unspoken obligation to consume the images, to watch the videos. It's easy to forget that activists are affected too."

Amid the protests and pressure associated with being a public figure, Packnett finds herself still needing to take a break and unplug from the rest of the world. "I finally learned when to genuinely disconnect. Yes, I know I'll be coming back to tragedy and sadness, but at least when I do I'll be coming back on a full tank instead of nearly empty."

Williams acknowledges that even the most experienced therapists can lack the cultural understanding necessary to treat minorities who exhibit symptoms of race-based trauma. The key, she says, is seeking help from culturally competent professionals or even loved ones. July marks Black Mental Health month and the Association of Black Psychologists have released guidelines for African-Americans experiencing cultural trauma from recent coverage of racial tension in the media and online.

April Reign says the first step is simply recognizing when racism and the deaths of minorities played out publicly is becoming overwhelming.

"Recognize that if you're numb, that means something. If you're breaking down in tears, that means something," she says. "It affects you more than you know, and there is nothing wrong with saying that this pains you. Understand it, and actively move toward healing yourself."

3

The Online Face of Political Outrage

Yemisi Akinbobola

Yemisi Akinbobola is an award-winning scholar and journalist. Her research focuses on media entrepreneurship, digital journalism, and African feminism.

In this viewpoint, Yemisi Akinbobola explores the potential and the limitations of feminist political mobilization in Africa. She focuses specifically on the manner in which online networks have encouraged a growing sense of outrage over widespread sexual violence in many African countries. Online platforms have allowed greater organization and mobilization of movements in addition to promoting the spread of information. However, she also asserts that bridging the gap between online engagement and public action is easier said than done.

K ill me, kill me, you people should just kill me." Those were the words of an unidentified woman as she was being gang raped by five men and her ordeal was filmed with one of their mobile phones. The crime is believed to have taken place at a private off-campus hostel near Abia State University, Nigeria, in August 2011.

The video of the rape, uploaded onto the Internet, caught the attention of blogger Linda Ikeji. Her subsequent blogpost of the crime sparked widespread anger and debate in Nigeria and beyond,

"Social Media Stimulates Nigerian Debate on Sexual Violence," by Yemisi Akinbobola, United Nations Africa Renewal. Reprinted by permission.

especially among bloggers, Twitter users and organizations such as the youth group EnoughisEnough Nigeria.

The authorities' initially dismissive response to the rape video fuelled the outrage. Assistant Commissioner of Police J.G. Micloth released a statement saying that after watching the video, he had determined that the victim had not resisted, nor could the suspects be identified from the "legs shown in the video amongst 70 million males in Nigeria."

The only positive reaction by the authorities came from Minister of Youth Development Mallam Bolaji Abdullahi, who described the rapists as "decadent and barbaric" and urged the authorities of Abia State University (ABSU) to investigate the crime.

Abike Dabiri, a member of the House of Assembly and the only prominent female politician to speak out publicly against the rape, attempted to raise the issue in the legislature. But she was rebuked by another parliamentarian who accused her of dabbling "into cases the police can handle" and asked that she "take up the case personally and not bring it to public glare."

Human rights lawyer Caroline Ajie and other campaigners expressed their disappointment at the lack of response from the first lady "to issue a tacit statement and lead in condemning the dastardly act." Ironically, the first lady is the founder of the Women for Change Initiative, which aims to raise women's awareness of their human rights and promote issues that affect Nigerian women and girls.

Unreported Crime

A majority of cases of sexual violence in Nigeria go unreported. This is due largely to fear on the part of the victim of being socially stigmatized or blamed. Ms. Ajie estimates that at least 2 million Nigerian girls experience sexual abuse annually and that only 28 per cent of rape cases are reported. Of those, only 12 per cent result in convictions.

Elsie Reed, founder of Delta Women, an organization that aims to empower and fight for the rights of women in Delta State, estimates that 80 per cent of Nigerian women have experienced some form of sexual harassment.

Marianne Møllmann, senior policy adviser at Amnesty International in London adds that violence against women, particularly sexual violence, is often viewed as normal or inevitable in many countries. "I've spoken to women whom I've asked if their husband is violent, and they say 'yeah, he rapes me sometimes,' as though it's normal," she says. "That shouldn't be."

According to the UN Women campaign against gender-based violence, Africa Unite, anywhere between 13 per cent and 45 per cent of women in sub-Saharan Africa experience assault by an "intimate partner during their lifetime."

Africa Unite also reports that in Uganda, for example, an astonishing 59 per cent of women between the ages of 15 and 49 "have experienced physical and/or sexual intimate partner violence in their lifetime."

Letty Chiwara, chief of the Africa Division of UN Women, explains that one of the key elements of the Africa Unite campaign is "to advocate or to make governments realize the need to have laws and policies that not only are about prevention, but are also about protecting and providing services to the victims."

Stirring Online Debate

The existence of video evidence of the 'ABSU rape', as it has become popularly known, added to the outrage at the lack of an appropriate response by the Nigerian authorities.

"Rape goes on in this country in universities everywhere," argues blogger Joachim MacEbong. "Many are not reported, those that are reported are waved away. So if such a video [shows] there was clearly no consent, and we cannot do anything about it, it doesn't make any sense."

Bloggers like Joachim have been at the forefront of the online debate regarding the ABSU rape. Popular Twitter users have also capitalized on their large following by releasing regular tweets to keep the debate alive.

Henry Okelue, who lives in Nigeria and has more than 3,000 Twitter followers, sent out periodic tweets in his contribution to the campaign. "[I was] trying to get people to focus on the issue, trying to help people to form an opinion on what had happened," he said. "Because the moment people stop talking about it, that's the end of it."

"Rape Walk"

On 5 October, less than three weeks after Ms. Ikeji first blogged about the ABSU rape, the social media campaign moved offline as campaigners went on a "rape walk" in Lagos and Abia. A similar walk was planned in Abuja, but had to be cancelled after authorities in the federal capital warned that the safety of the campaigners could not be guaranteed.

In Lagos, only about 60 people were present at the march, suggesting perhaps that campaigners still have a long way to go in establishing physical social mobilization in their efforts to combat sexual violence against women.

However, the use of virtual platforms to open up the debate is beginning to yield some positive results, according to Ms. Reed. "People now come forward, and people talk about it, and people are now aware that it's not okay to sexually harass somebody."

Yet, despite the assertive social media campaign and the subsequent "rape walk," no one has been charged in the ABSU rape.

4

The Tribal Roots of Modern Political Outrage

Jonathan Haidt

A moral psychologist and professor of ethics at New York University's Stern School of Business, Jonathan Haidt's research focuses on the emotional and anthropological dimensions of moral issues.

In this excerpted viewpoint, the moral psychologist Jonathan Haidt explores the notion that moral conflict in the public sphere may be inevitable because of the tribal orientation of human psychology. In asserting this, he suggests that public outrage is not simply a result of the current political climate, but a part of human nature. In fact, this tribal aspect of human nature was accounted for by the Founding Fathers in the Constitution.

When we look back at the ways our ancestors lived, there's no getting around it: we are tribal primates. We are exquisitely designed and adapted by evolution for life in small societies with intense, animistic religion and violent intergroup conflict over territory. We love tribal living so much that we invented sports, fraternities, street gangs, fan clubs, and tattoos. Tribalism is in our hearts and minds. We'll never stamp it out entirely, but we can minimize its effects because we are a behaviorally flexible species. We can live in many different ways, from egalitarian hunter-gatherer groups of 50 individuals to feudal hierarchies binding together millions. And in the last two centuries, a lot of us have lived in

"The Age of Outrage," by Jonathan Haidt, Manhattan Institute for Policy Research, Inc., previously published by City Journal, December 17, 2017. Reprinted by permission.

large, multi-ethnic secular liberal democracies. So clearly that is possible. *But how much margin of error do we have in such societies?*

Here is the fine-tuned liberal democracy hypothesis: as tribal primates, human beings are unsuited for life in large, diverse secular democracies, *unless* you get certain settings finely adjusted to make possible the development of stable political life. This seems to be what the Founding Fathers believed. Jefferson, Madison, and the rest of those eighteenth-century deists clearly *did* think that designing a constitution was like designing a giant clock, a clock that might run forever if they chose the right springs and gears.

Thankfully, our Founders were good psychologists. They knew that we are not angels; they knew that we are tribal creatures. As Madison wrote in *Federalist 10*: "the latent causes of faction are thus sown in the nature of man." Our Founders were also good historians; they were well aware of Plato's belief that democracy is the second worst form of government because it inevitably decays into tyranny. Madison wrote in *Federalist 10* about pure or direct democracies, which he said are quickly consumed by the passions of the majority: "such democracies have ever been spectacles of turbulence and contention … and have in general been as short in their lives as they have been violent in their deaths."

So what did the Founders do? They built in safeguards against runaway factionalism, such as the division of powers among the three branches, and an elaborate series of checks and balances. But they also knew that they had to train future generations of clock mechanics. They were creating a new kind of republic, which would demand far more maturity from its citizens than was needed in nations ruled by a king or other Leviathan.

[…]

Why do we hate and fear each other so much more than we used to as recently as the early 1990s? […] Imagine three kids making a human chain with their arms, and one kid has his free hand wrapped around a pole. The kids start running around in a circle, around the pole, faster and faster. The centrifugal force increases. That's the force pulling outward as the human centrifuge speeds up. But at the same time, the kids strengthen their grip. That's the centripetal force, pulling them inward along the chain of their arms. Eventually the centrifugal force exceeds the centripetal force and their hands slip. The chain breaks. This, I believe, is what is happening to our country. I'll briefly mention five of the trends that Abrams and I identified, all of which can be seen as increasing centrifugal forces or weakening centripetal forces.

- *External enemies*: Fighting and winning two world wars, followed by the Cold War, had an enormous unifying effect. The Vietnam War was different, but in general, war is the strongest known centripetal force. Since 1989, we have had no unifying common enemy.

- *The media*: Newspapers in the early days of the republic were partisan and often quite nasty. But with the advent of television in the mid-twentieth century, America experienced something unusual: the media was a gigantic centripetal force. Americans got much of their news from three television networks, which were regulated and required to show political balance. That couldn't last, and it began to change in the 1980s with the advent of cable TV and narrowcasting, followed by the Internet in the 1990s, and social media in the 2000s. Now we are drowning in outrage stories, very high-quality outrage stories, often supported by horrifying video clips. Social media is turning out to be a gigantic centrifugal force.

- *Immigration and diversity*: This one is complicated and politically fraught. Let me be clear that I think immigration and diversity are good things, overall. The economists seem to agree that immigration brings large economic benefits. The complete dominance of America in Nobel prizes, music, and the arts, and now the technology sector, would not have happened if we had not been open to immigrants. But as a social psychologist, I must point out that immigration and diversity have *many* sociological effects, some of which are negative. The main one is that they reduce social capital—the bonds of trust that exist between individuals. The political scientist Robert Putnam found this in a paper titled "E Pluribus Unum," in which he followed his data to a conclusion he clearly did not relish: "In the short run, immigration and ethnic diversity tend to reduce social solidarity and social capital. New evidence from the US suggests that in ethnically diverse neighborhoods residents of all races tend to 'hunker down.' Trust (even of one's own race) is lower, altruism and community cooperation rarer, friends fewer." In short, despite its other benefits, diversity is a centrifugal force, something the Founders were well aware of. In *Federalist 2*, John Jay wrote that we should count it as a blessing that America possessed "one united people—a people descended from the same ancestors, the same language, professing the same religion." I repeat that diversity has many good effects too, and I am grateful that America took in my grandparents from Russia and Poland, and my wife's parents from Korea. But Putnam's findings make it clear that those who want more diversity should be even *more* attentive to strengthening centripetal forces.

The final two causes I will mention are likely to arouse the most disagreement, because these are the two where I blame specific parties, specific sides. They are: the Republicans in Washington, and the Left on campus. Both have strengthened the centrifugal forces that are now tearing us apart.

- *The more radical Republican Party*: When the Democrats ran the House of Representatives for almost all of six decades, before 1995, they did not treat the Republican minority particularly well. So I can understand Newt Gingrich's desire for revenge when he took over as Speaker of the House in 1995. But many of the changes he made polarized the Congress, made bipartisan cooperation more difficult, and took us into a new era of outrage and conflict in Washington. One change stands out to me, speaking as a social psychologist: he changed the legislative calendar so that all business was done Tuesday through Thursday, and he encouraged his incoming freshmen *not* to move to the District. He did not *want* them to develop personal friendships with Democrats. He did not *want* their spouses to serve on the same charitable boards. But personal relationships among legislators and their families in Washington had long been a massive centripetal force. Gingrich deliberately weakened it. And this all happened along with the rise of Fox News. Many political scientists have noted that Fox News and the right-wing media ecosystem had an effect on the Republican Party that is unlike anything that happened on the left. It rewards more extreme statements, more grandstanding, more outrage. Many people will point out that the media leans left overall, and that the Democrats did some polarizing things, too. Fair enough. But it is clear that Gingrich set out to create a more partisan, zero-sum Congress, and he succeeded. This more combative culture then filtered up to the Senate, and out to the rest of the Republican Party.

- *The new identity politics of the Left*: Jonathan Rauch offers a simple definition of identity politics: a "political mobilization organized around group characteristics such as race, gender, and sexuality, as opposed to party, ideology, or pecuniary interest." Rauch then adds: "In America, this sort of mobilization is not new, unusual, unAmerican, illegitimate, nefarious, or particularly leftwing." This definition makes it easy for us to identify two kinds of identity politics: the good kind is that which, in the long run, is a centripetal force. The bad kind is that which, in the long run, is a centrifugal force.

Injustice is centrifugal. It destroys trust and causes righteous anger. Institutionalized racism bakes injustice into the system and plants the seeds of an eventual explosion. When slavery was written into the Constitution, it set us up for the greatest explosion of our history. It was a necessary explosion, but we didn't manage the healing process well in the Reconstruction era. When Jim Crow was written into Southern laws, it led to another period of necessary explosions, in the 1960s.

The civil rights struggle was indeed identity politics, but it was an effort to fix a mistake, to make us better and stronger as a nation. Martin Luther King's rhetoric made it clear that this was a campaign to create conditions that would allow national reconciliation. He drew on the moral resources of the American civil religion to activate our shared identity and values: "When the architects of our republic wrote the magnificent words of the Constitution and the Declaration of Independence, they were signing a promissory note." And: "I still have a dream. It is a dream deeply rooted in the American dream. I have a dream that one day this nation will rise up and live out the true meaning of its creed: 'We hold these truths to be self-evident, that all men are created equal.'"

Of course, some people saw the civil rights movement as divisive, or centrifugal. But King's speech is among the most famous in American history precisely because *it framed our greatest moral failing as an opportunity for centripetal redemption*. This is what I'm calling the good kind of identity politics.

Let us contrast King's identity politics with the version taught in universities today. There is a new variant that has swept through the academy in the last five years. It is called intersectionality. The term and concept were presented in a 1989 essay by Kimberlé Crenshaw, a law professor at UCLA, who made the very reasonable point that a black woman's experience in America is not captured by the summation of the black experience and the female experience. She analyzed a legal case in which black women were victims of discrimination at General Motors, even when the company could show that it hired plenty of blacks (in factory jobs dominated by men), and it hired plenty of women (in clerical jobs dominated by whites). So even though GM was found not guilty of discriminating against blacks or women, it ended up hiring hardly any black women. This is an excellent argument. What academic could oppose the claim that when analyzing a complex system, we must look at interaction effects, not just main effects?

But what happens when young people study intersectionality? In some majors, it's woven into many courses. Students memorize diagrams showing matrices of privilege and oppression. It's not just white privilege causing black oppression, and male privilege causing female oppression; its heterosexual vs. LGBTQ, able-bodied vs. disabled; young vs. old, attractive vs. unattractive, even fertile vs. infertile. Anything that a group has that is good or valued is seen as a kind of privilege, which causes a kind of oppression in those who don't have it. A funny thing happens when you take young human beings, whose minds evolved for tribal warfare and us/them thinking, and you fill those minds full of binary dimensions. You tell them that one side of each binary is good and the other is bad. You turn on their ancient tribal circuits, preparing them for battle. Many students find it thrilling; it floods them with a sense of meaning and purpose.

And here's the strategically brilliant move made by intersectionality: all of the binary dimensions of oppression are said to be interlocking and overlapping. America is said to be one giant matrix of oppression, and its victims cannot fight their battles separately. They must all come together to fight their common enemy, the group that sits at the top of the pyramid of oppression: the straight, white, cis-gendered, able-bodied Christian or Jewish or possibly atheist male. This is why a perceived slight against one victim group calls forth protest from all victim groups. This is why so many campus groups now align against Israel. Intersectionality is like NATO for social-justice activists.

This means that on any campus where intersectionality thrives, conflict will be eternal, because no campus can eliminate all offense, all microaggressions, and all misunderstandings. This is why the use of shout-downs, intimidation, and even violence in response to words and ideas is most common at our most progressive universities, in the most progressive regions of the country. It's schools such as Yale, Brown, and Middlebury in New England, and U.C. Berkeley, Evergreen, and Reed on the West Coast. Are those the places where oppression is worst, or are they the places where this new way of thinking is most widespread?

[...]

5

Political Outrage in the Media

Jeffrey M. Berry and Sarah Sobieraj

Jeffrey M. Berry is the John Richard Skuse Professor of Political Science at Tufts University. Sarah Sobieraj is an associate professor of sociology at Tufts University. Their collaborative research focuses on political outrage in the media.

In this viewpoint, Berry and Sobieraj explore the appeal of "outrage talk"—why audiences, especially conservative ones, gravitate toward the intensity and incivility of the contemporary American political discourse. They assert that there is a correlation between increased discomfort toward engaging in public political conversations and increased viewership of outrage-based political news programs. While there is a large demand for outrage-based media outlets, the impact they have on political discourse may have a negative effect on US politics in general.

Pundits regularly bemoan "incivility" in American politics, but the coarseness of political discourse has moved far beyond mere incivility, generally understood as showing lack of respect. The acrimony and intensity of much political speech and behavior today is best understood as outrage talk—political speech that uses theatrical rhetorical tactics such as ad hominem attacks, slippery-slope argumentation, belittling and mockery in an effort to provoke

"The Roots and Impact of Outrage-Mongering in U.S. Political-Opinion Media: Research Brief," by Jeffrey M. Berry and Sarah Sobieraj, Journalist's Resource, October 28, 2014. https://journalistsresource.org/studies/society/news-media/outrage-mongering-in-u-s-political-opinion-media. Licensed under CC BY-ND 4.0. © 2019 the Shorenstein Center.

emotional responses from the audience such as anger, fear and moral indignation.

Outrage Talk Is Rampant

Deliberately inflammatory political speech is ubiquitous on talk radio, cable news analysis shows and popular political blogs— whether it is *Hardball's* Chris Matthews calling Senator Ted Cruz a "terrorist" who wants to "destroy ... American government" or Glenn Beck saying on his radio program that President Obama is a "Marxist revolutionary," outrage-mongering is a genre of political media that has grown exponentially in the last 20 years.

Content analysis of 13 variants of outrage in 10 top-rated shows on cable news, 10 top-rated shows on talk radio and 20 widely read political blogs revealed a staggering number of outrage incidents. Fully 100% of the cable news analysis episodes contained outrage, while close to 90% of radio shows and roughly 80% of blog entries were characterized by outrage. What's more, many individual episodes or posts included dozens of incidents. On the Fox and MSNBC shows that dominate the cable news-analysis landscape, outrage talk happens roughly every other minute during airtime not devoted to commercial advertisements.

Stoking Outrage Is a Business Strategy

Polarization in society and politics is not an adequate explanation for the growing cadre of media hosts deploying outrage talk to stoke the emotions of their viewers, listeners, and readers. Indeed, polarization in elections and legislatures may be as much symptom as cause. The ascent of outrage says more about changing media technologies and regulatory guidelines and the broader culture than it does about the political views of most citizens.

Various changes have coalesced to make scream politics a lucrative, sound business strategy. Media regulation has been reduced, freeing outlets to say almost anything. Cable television multiplies outlets competing to grab eyeballs and ears in their own niches. And political life has become intensely personally focused.

Together, these shifts encourage media strategies unimaginable even 20 years ago, when outlets used pleasant and inoffensive content to appeal to the broadest possible audiences. Nowadays, controversial, attention-grabbing content helps to draw an audience in a cluttered media landscape characterized by seemingly limitless options.

Nielsen, Arbitron and other organizations charged with measuring media audiences suggest that the daily aggregate audience for programming featuring political outrage is 47 million Americans. Talk radio attracts the largest audience, with right-wing host Rush Limbaugh alone reaching some 14 million listeners a week. Close to 4,000 radio stations broadcast an all-talk format, triple the number in existence 15 years ago. Talk radio is much more successful with conservative audiences than with progressive listeners, especially political talk radio, the audience for which is 90% conservative.

Why Are Audiences Attracted— Especially Conservatives?

What do audiences find appealing about outrage media? Through in-depth interviews with self-identified fans, we learned that these offerings function as safe havens for audience members increasingly uncomfortable with real-world political conversations. Face-to-face political talk generates fears of social rejection, social conflict and the potential embarrassment of looking ill-informed, but people escape these worries when they listen to or watch charismatic hosts of outrage-based programs that help the viewer feel included. Hosts typically do this for their audiences by proffering pseudo-friendships, by flattering fans for their work ethic, moral judgment and intellect, and by telling their audiences that they are informed people armed with "the truth."

The function of outrage-spreading programs as personal safe havens may help explain why conservatives are dominant in this genre. Our interviews reveal that conservative fans feel they take a greater social risk when talking about politics with others, because their policy preferences—and they themselves—can end up being labeled "racist" in an era where intolerance is stigmatized in most public settings. In light of such risks, conservatives find political-media spaces for political "conversation" particularly valuable, places where feelings they may have can be aired and expressed without rebuke.

We measured the incidence of outrage-based talk on left-leaning and right-leaning political media outlets. For programs with relatively low levels of outrage—two to five incidents per program—left-leaning and right-leaning programs or blog postings are roughly equal. But when it comes to programs or posts that invoke outrage more frequently, the outlets lean conservative, especially programs or posts with 50 or more expressions of outrage per episode.

Broader Damage to American Politics

For individual Americans, watching or listening to outrage talk may undermine tolerance, promote misunderstandings of public issues, and make politics seem unappealing. But damage is also visited on the US political system as a whole when political opinion hosts incessantly stigmatize collaboration and compromise. When legislators enter into bipartisan negotiations they are often denounced on air as unprincipled sell-outs; and outrage-oriented outlets regularly boost primary-election candidates who challenge moderates, or even otherwise orthodox legislators, who compromise. Many politicians conclude it might be better to do nothing than to work on difficult governing decisions, especially those that require bipartisan cooperation.

6

#MeToo and the Trump Presidency: Are They Related?

Ashwini Tambe

Ashwini Tambe is an associate professor of women's studies at the University of Maryland and Editorial Director of the journal Feminist Studies.

In this viewpoint, Ashwini Tambe examines the recent political mobilization of American women (exemplified by the Women's March and the #MeToo movement) in the context of President Trump's election. She makes the argument that many women's anger has been triggered by President Trump's election, and while they often feel powerless to take on the issue of Trump's alleged sexual misconduct, they are more empowered to take down perpetrators of sexual misconduct in their own lives.

The cascade of sexual harassment accusations over the past month has moved from high-profile men to lesser-known people in sectors such as higher education and the restaurant industry. In an important and fundamental way, the ground beneath us has shifted: Victims everywhere have lost their patience and their fear, and are finding willing listeners.

A question worth asking is: Why has it shifted now?

#MeToo and Beyond

The current outpouring of allegations may seem sudden, but it isn't surprising if you've been tracking the massive swell in women's activism over the past year, as women's studies scholars like me are doing.

Yes, the viral #MeToo campaign has been instrumental in raising this issue. According to Facebook, nearly half the people in the United States are friends with someone who posted a message about experiences of assault or harassment. But #MeToo draws its steam from other collective efforts. Even before #MeToo, the 3-million-strong private Facebook group Pantsuit Nation, founded just before Election Day 2016, witnessed hundreds of thousands of women breaking their silence about gender-based violence, among other topics. The Women's March on Jan. 21 was the largest single-day globally coordinated public gathering in world history.

Over the past year, there's been a clear spike in the number of US women running for political office. Emily's List reported that in 2017, more than 16,000 women expressed interest in running, compared to the 920 women who did so in 2015 and 2016 combined.

I would argue there's a single thread running through all these phenomena: a fierce outrage about the election of Donald Trump.

Women activists are, of course, responding to a range of economic, social and political issues that a Trump presidency raises. But one of the most galling provocations is that Trump acknowledged being a sexual predator and faced no actual consequences. He was recorded saying that he used his star status to forcibly kiss and grab women—and still ascended to the White House. He has been accused of sexual assault three times—by an ex-wife, business associate and a minor—in lawsuits that were later withdrawn. Sixteen women have accused him of sexual harassment. In my opinion, the reason none of these accusations has gathered traction is because of competing news cycle distractions and the pressures his accusers face.

For many, Trump represents the ultimate unpunished sexual predator. Right after the election, therapists and counseling centers were reportedly flooded with patients—especially women patients—seeking help with stress and processing past sexual traumas. Now, one year into the Trump administration, with the ballast provided by women's feverish organizing and the instant power of social media, I see the initial anxious response to the election mutating into something else: a collective emboldening. Even if victims of sexual predation cannot affect this presidency, they can try to fix other problems. Trump has made the comeuppance of other powerful men feel more urgent.

There's a sociological concept that captures what's afoot: "horizontal violence." This term describes situations where people turn on people in their own lives when provoked by forces beyond their control. The Brazilian philosopher Paolo Freire used the term in 1968 to describe substituting a difficult powerful target with a more accessible one like peers or kin. Those who use horizontal violence are typically members of oppressed groups without easy access to economic resources or institutional channels of expression such as the law or the media. One example is when low-income men who are experiencing job instability take out their frustration on intimate partners.

It is, of course, inaccurate to term what sexual harassment victims are doing "violence," so a better term in this situation might be "horizontal action." It is also true that most allegations involve men who have greater power than their victims; in this sense, the action is not exactly horizontal. Nonetheless, the fact that victims are naming their colleagues in such great numbers suggests an awakening: They no longer want to protect their professions and careers nor play along with open secrets. It feels important to topple those perpetrators within reach. Trump's impunity has, I suggest, provoked the impatience and fury at the heart of this movement.

This speculation is, of course, hard to prove, since the private injuries of victims can sufficiently explain the anger they feel. Victims who have spoken out might not openly describe Trump as the first cause for their frustration or bravery. But the frequency with which Trump is described as a trigger is telling. We need to theorize, on a cultural scale, why this collective disruption has happened now rather than, say, two years ago, when Bill Cosby was accused by multiple women, or last year, when Roger Ailes was deposed.

As we dissect the implications of what some call "the Weinstein effect," I suggest we notice something else in the very air we breathe: a deep frustration that a self-confessed sexual predator remains—thus far—immune.

7

A Backlash Against the Trump Administration

Dave Davies

Dave Davies is a radio journalist for WHYY in Philadelphia and a columnist for the Philadelphia Daily News. *He has covered both local and national politics for over thirty years.*

In this viewpoint, Dave Davies explores the idea of electoral backlash: when a particular political faction achieves tremendous power, there is often a surge of energy among the opposition, which ultimately limits the ability of those in power to act unilaterally. While this tends to inspire greater political involvement from those in the opposition party, the extent to which it will impact future elections is variable.

President Donald Trump's inauguration a year ago was a triumph for his one-of-a-kind campaign, and a call to action for many Democrats who resolved to become more politically active.

Did it make a difference?

Absolutely. It's clear the "Trump bump" of progressive enthusiasm had an impact on Democratic fortunes in the Philadelphia region last year, and will continue to affect local politics in 2018.

Whether it's enough of a movement to capture some Republican congressional seats in the suburbs remains to be seen.

"Outrage Over Trump Is Helping Democrats Win Elections," by Dave Davies, WHYY, January 16, 2018. Reprinted by permission.

Loud Out of the Gate

The day after his swearing-in, an estimated 50,000 people came out for a women's march in Philadelphia protesting the Trump presidency.

It was unclear whether that energy would translate into the stuff that wins elections—volunteers, contributions, and votes.

David Landau, chairman of Delaware County's Democratic party said he saw a difference right away.

"We have literally thousands of people, including most of our candidates [for county office] who woke up on November 9th and just said, 'I'm part of the problem that elected Donald Trump, because I haven't been active, and I need to do something,'" Landau said.

Four months after Trump's inauguration, progressives in Philadelphia staged a stunning upset, when first-time candidate Rebecca Rhynhart captured the City Controller's office by upsetting three-term incumbent Alan Butkovitz in the Democratic Party primary.

Progressives also turned out in numbers to vote for District Attorney candidate Larry Krasner, the beneficiary of more than $1.4 million in campaign spending by billionaire George Soros.

A few days after the primary, City Commissioner Al Schmidt compared turnout by age group to results in the primary four years earlier.

"Among the youngest age cohort, or millennial voters, their participation increased by nearly 300 percent, from about 9,000 to around 34,000 voters," Schmidt said.

While millennial turnout was still only ten percent, it was a surge that made a difference.

But would the Democratic momentum carry another six months into the general election?

It appears it did.

Blue Counties

In Delaware County, where Democrats had never won a seat on the county council, they beat Republicans for the two contested seats and three other offices. They also captured some township and borough posts in the county, where Republicans had dominated for decades.

Democrats also had historic wins in Chester and Bucks Counties, making for a blue tide in the Philadelphia suburbs.

Chester County Democratic Chairman Brian McGuiness said there were enthusiastic new candidates, and voters determined to use local elections to send a national message.

"People can say what they want, but Trump was on the ballot, and his policies were on the ballot," McGuiness said the day after the election. "We wanted to make this a statement election."

A National Impact?

The suburban counties where Democrats got those wins comprise big parts of three Congressional seats held by Republicans that the national Democratic party hopes to capture this year: the 8th District, held by Rep. Brian Fitzpatrick, the 6th, held by Rep. Ryan Costello, and the 7th congressional seat, which Rep. Pat Meehan took from the Democrats in 2010.

Landau, the chair of Delco Democrats, said the emergence of new candidates and gains in county and local offices will matter in the races to come.

"This election is a pathway to 2018," Landau said. "It allows us to set up the infrastructure, show our success, and creates both the perception and the reality that we can take back the 7th Congressional District, and pick up a few more state house seats and state senate seats."

Are Republicans worried?

GOP media strategist John Brabender said he's concerned about the Democratic surge in the counties, but it's way too early to write off Republicans in those three congressional seats.

Brabender said Meehan, Costello, and Fitzpatrick have plenty of local support, and he noted that in 2016, they got more votes than the president in their districts.

"Despite Donald Trump either barely winning their districts or not winning their district, they won by double digits last time," Brabender said.

Local Races in 2018

Besides congressional races, there's a crop of first-time Democratic candidates seeking local offices, such as party committee posts and seats in the state legislature.

North Philadelphia activist Malcolm Kenyatta is running for State Representative. He said those who predicted the anti-Trump wave would peter out are in for a surprise in 2018.

"I remember people saying to me, 'Well, this engagement won't last.' I remember people interviewing me about 'engagement fatigue," Kenyatta said. "Not only do I not see it slowing down, but I see it picking up."

Many of those progressive candidates for local seats will run not against Republicans, but against incumbent Democrats.

It's not yet clear how many will actually file to run. The deadline is March 6.

8

Occupy and the Reemergence of Leftist Mass Movements

Dan La Botz

Dan La Botz is a writer, teacher, and activist based in Cincinnati, Ohio. He was involved in the Occupy Cincinnati movement.

In this viewpoint, a former Occupy activist discusses the impact the movement has had on the political landscape, particularly for the Left. He claims it is a sign that young leftists are beginning to organize around social, political, and economic issues in a way that's reminiscent of the movements of the 1960s and 1970s. He argues that although the movement did not reach the heights of earlier political movements, it suggests a renewed interest in political organization among young people and the possibility of a populist, socialist-leaning movement in the future.

The Occupy movement has changed the American political landscape. We are at the opening of a new mass movement and a radicalization that presage an era of coming social upheaval and class conflict that require the left to both analyze these developments and to develop a strategy to intervene. The left today, small, divided, and weak, must develop an approach that will make it possible for it to grow and unite so that it can influence events. The developments taking place are somewhat episodic and uneven, but they have a common character, that of a mass,

"From Occupy Wall Street to Occupy the World: The Emergence of a Mass Movement," by Dan La Botz, New Politics at newpol.org, 2012. Reprinted by permission.

populist, leftward moving force. Our task is to help that force to grow and to help its inherently radical character to fully emerge and to become self-consciously anti-capitalist and an eventually socialist movement. To do so we must respect both the movement's character and the convictions of its participants. We must share the work of the movement and enter its conversation prepared not only to share our view, but also to learn from others.

A handful of young people started Occupy Wall Street in mid-September, as a protest against the banks and corporations that have grown rich while most Americans have grown poorer. Responding to the call to occupy Wall Street by *Adbusters*, the Canadian anti-consumerism magazine, they took Zuccotti Park on September 17 and began a permanent encampment. Within weeks they had attracted hundreds and then thousands to marches and demonstration in New York City—one of them leading to the arrest of hundreds on the Brooklyn Bridge. The movement's chant "We are the 99 percent" rang out not only in the Wall Street canyon but also across the country. Soon there were scores of Occupy groups across the United States camping out in public places, marching and rallying in cities and towns against corporate greed. By mid-October the Occupy movement had spread to every continent, to dozens of countries, and to hundreds of cities.

The movement and its repression are having profound ramifications in the working class. State and local governments responded to the movement with police repression resulting in the arrest of 3,000 activists in a dozen cities in the first weeks. The police, on foot and mounted, sometimes formed in phalanxes, and wearing riot gear, have raided the Occupy encampments using pepper spray, clubs, tear gas, and stun grenades. The assault on the Oakland camp led to the shooting of Iraqi war veteran Scott Olsen. In response an Occupy Oakland meeting of 3,000 called for a general strike, a call that led to mass demonstrations, the closing of the Port of Oakland and of many schools. While many of us, myself included, had believed that a new union movement would arise from struggles in the plants and in the unions themselves, the impact of Occupy suggests that many union officials see Occupy as a social force that can strengthen the union movement and that workers responding to Occupy may be emboldened to break the stranglehold of bureaucracy as they respond to external developments.

We are witnessing the birth of the first major mass movement on the left in the United States since the decline of the leftist upsurge of the 1960s and early 1970s. While the new movement has not yet reached the proportions of the upheaval of forty years ago, when at times there were millions in the streets and hundreds of thousands of workers on strike, still it is clear that Occupy represents both a mass movement and a new radicalization. The Occupy Wall Street Declaration published on September 30 is a remarkable catalog of the grievances of the American people, touching on every issue from the economic crisis to the wars abroad, to the looming environmental catastrophe. While the movement cannot now be called anti-capitalist, not in the way that the anti-globalization protests of the 1990s and 2000s were, nevertheless, Occupy's populist, anti-corporate politics are infused with a profound radicalism expressed in its intense moral repugnance toward the existing system.

While some of the young people have been inspired by the occupation of Tahrir Square and by the *indignados* of Spain, this is an essentially American movement about American issues. The Occupy folks are furious at the corporations and many are angry at government as well; they are generally hostile to the Republicans and disappointed in the Democrats. Occupy is not anti-capitalist, but neither is it liberal. The Occupy activists have shown little interest in liberal organizations, the Democratic Party, political candidates, or liberal nostrums. Frustrated with the economic and political situation, they want to tax the rich, they want to stop the foreclosures, they want jobs for themselves and all the other unemployed. They demand an end to the wars in Iraq and Afghanistan. They want justice, not quite sure what that would look like or how to get there, but they are committed to the goal.

While most of those down at Zuccotti Park where the occupation is taking place are from New York, others have come in ones and twos from around the country to take a stand against corporate greed. Visitors are impressed with the organization: the kitchen, the medical center, the media center, the library, the daily lectures and appearances by intellectual luminaries such as Joseph Stiglitz, former chief economist of the World Bank; Jeffrey Sachs, Harvard professor and special advisor to the United Nations' secretary general; Barbara Ehrenreich, feminist and author; and philosopher and Princeton professor Cornell West. There is now also a newspaper, The *Occupied Wall Street Journal*, which is going national. Tens of thousands of dollars have been raised through small contributions by both Occupy Wall Street and the newspaper. While they may not have all of these structures, occupations in other cities have the kitchen or the library, or did until the police ran them out of the park, and most have some sort of educational program with classes on the banks, corporations and capitalism, but also on the history of social movements, and the arts and the movement.

The idealist youth who launched the movement soon found that they were occupying parks that had been occupied by the homeless for years. The encounter of professionals, workers, and students with the jobless and the homeless has given those who are somewhat better off an insight into poverty, alcoholism, and mental illness, allowed them to put a face on social misery, and it has brought about greater compassion. The movement has generally embraced the homeless. While their addictions or mental illness prevent some from participating in the Occupy movement and may even lead them to disrupt it, other homeless folk have been uplifted by the experience, joining in the debates and discussions and bringing the perspective of those who stand at the very bottom of the social heap.

"We the people ... have found our voice." So begin many of the general assemblies throughout the country. The general assembly is the life of the occupations, scores or hundreds of participants in the movement (not all directly engaged in the encampment) meeting to discuss the group's vision, principles, strategy, and tactics. The rotation of facilitators, the open discussion, the generally amicable debate, the consensus model of decision making all reflect the movement's commitment to direct democracy. The hand signals with the wiggling fingers—up for yes, out in front for on the fence, down for no, crossed arms and fists for a moral rejection of the proposal—draw everyone into participation in the discussion. The human mic, that is, the repetition of a speaker's words because the law forbids electric amplification equipment in the parks, is a powerful tool and a striking symbol of the idea of the collective voice. People listen more carefully, and, repeating the speakers' words, really hear them, hear them twice, hear them magnified by themselves as they spread over the crowd. If the discussions are sometimes tedious, frustrating, or silly, they are at other times inspiring, and no assembly passes without some person, new to activism, standing up and giving a testimonial that reaffirms the significance of the movement.

The occupation's work is done through face-to-face and virtual committee meetings. The leaders of the leaderless movement, as it sees itself, are in most places a constantly changing constellation of activists of all ages and often of great diversity in other respects as well. Important decisions generally come back to the general assembly for approval, but autonomous actions take place initiated by small bands of occupiers.

Occupy is both a real movement of thousands on the street and a virtual movement of millions on the social media. The movement's voice and its images are posted on local Occupy websites, on Facebook pages, on YouTube, shared on Twitter. Thousands "like" the posts, or comment on them, or add their own photo or video. The activists participating in the occupations, demonstrations, and marches follow the development of their local movement and of the national movement on their smart phones or other electronic devices even as they occupy. Text messages summon up flash-mobs for quickie actions, and photos taken with cell phones immediately tell the world what happened.

Occupy Wall Street and its offspring, nearly all of which began with white youth, have grown not only larger, but also more diverse, attracting people from all walks of life and every segment of the society. They are making real their chant, "This is what democracy looks like." In Atlanta and some other cities, African Americans and Latinos have taken up the occupation. In Albuquerque—where Indians and Mexicans feel they have been occupied by imperial powers for so long—they call it (Un)occupy. But the sentiment is the same: the country's on the wrong track. Even where the participation of people of color in the occupation is not proportional and may be small, still bonds of solidarity are established that cross the lines of ethnicity, race, religion, language and culture. On the borders north and south, people cross the line to join the occupation on the other side.

Utopian and Inspiring

Occupy is in part a coming together of activists from other movements. Watching any of the demonstrations in any city on any day one sees pass by on the t-shirts and jackets all the logos of every movement that has touched the country in the last decade: anti-war, LGBTQ, foreclosures, and civil rights activists. Walking among them are others new to the movement, blue collar and white collar workers, so far without their logos, carrying their own hand painted signs with slogans like "Create Jobs, Reform Wall Street, Tax the Wealthy More," and "The People are Too Big to Fail." One sign down at Wall Street read, "This is the First Time I've Felt Hopeful in a Very Long Time."

The movement has a utopian character. Many of those involved in it want not only to overcome the immediate effects of the economic crisis—they want a better life, a better country, a better world. The movement as such has no ideology. This is populism of a left wing sort: the people versus big business and bad government. Though there are anarchists in it and they have given it some of their style, it is not an anarchist movement. Though there are some socialists in it, the movement as a whole is by no means socialist. And while the movement is anti-corporate, it would be going too far to claim that it is anti-capitalist, at least not yet. All over the country one sees three flags flying—the American flag, the anarchist black flag, and the socialist red flag—a phenomenon expressing not so much confusion or competition as the interaction of the people who hold the various political philosophies suggested by these banners. Occupy is an endless discussion, a continuous conversation, a generally good-willed political debate. What is perhaps best and most exciting about the movement is the confluence of the many social movements with middle class and working class people and poor people who have come down to Wall Street or in some other town or city down to Main Street to say, "We've had it." The utopianism of the movement has inspired ordinary people to say, "We can live differently, we must, and we will."

The movement has imposed its own ethos and sense of decorum on the group. We see a rebirth of civility. Mutual respect is highly valued. Egotistical behavior, the pushing of personal agendas and what are perceived as inappropriate invasions of the space are frowned upon. The group's norms have inhibited leftist organizations and activists who generally do not identify themselves as members of this or that organization and generally do not sell their newspapers and magazines at the occupations. The longstanding practice of some socialist missionaries who stood and announced that they came from a particular party that published such and such a newspaper has disappeared, except among the most hardened and irrelevant sects.

To some extent, the implicit strictures against propagandizing for socialism reflect both the anarchist and liberal strains in politics. This raises the question of how socialists should express their views, distribute their literature, and recruit to their organizations.

Most socialists have found themselves principally joining in the discussion, trying to show how the ideals of Occupy find their fulfillment in an anti-capitalist and pro-socialist position. But it isn't easy. The general assembly and the human mic don't really facilitate the presentation of complex ideas and analysis, or the development of program and strategy. Leftist newspapers are distributed discreetly and potential recruits are invited off-site to talk. Virtually all the socialist organizations see Occupy as the beginning of something big, though none of us has a full-developed strategy for the movement. Nor should we; this is a movement in the making and it is as important to join in and learn from it as it is to attempt to help provide leadership for it.

The Occupy movement has done what in other countries at other times has been done by the labor unions or by labor or socialist parties: it has expressed the grievances of the people and attempted to speak for them, for the 99 percent. Occupy is a kind of a party, not a party with a formal structure, but potential peoples party in formation, the party of working people, the party of the poor, the party of the dispossessed, the oppressed, and the exploited. The Occupy movement excoriates the banks, the corporations, the economic elite, the 1 percent with their greed, and it criticizes the government for its complicity and its corruption. Occupy is the moralizing party of the people, asking the people to recognize themselves in it, to join it, and to make real its claim to represent the 99 percent.

A month or so into the Occupy movement, the labor unions began to take an interest. In New York the unions turned out thousands of their members for a major march in October. At about the same time, Richard Trumka, head of the AFL-CIO, spoke out in favor of the movement, as did leaders of various national and local unions. Yet the AFL-CIO and the Occupy movement remain wary of each other. The AFL-CIO's principal goal in the next year is to help Obama and the Democrats win the November 2012 elections, and both the AFL-CIO and the Democrats would love to figure out how to harness Occupy for their political and electoral goals. Many in the Occupy movement would love to have more workers involved, the unions involved, but they fear the labor bureaucracy's heavy hand. And, more important for some, they fear losing their political independence to union officials and Democrats.

The labor movement's formal endorsement of Occupy has made it possible for union activists in New York and some other cities to use the rise of the new movement as a way to engage with their unions and to encourage their fellow union members to take action. For example, activists from Occupy Wall Street joined Teamster Local 814 members in protesting at a Sotheby's auction because of the company lockout of 43 workers. In many cities, at least some of the labor unions and their members have come down to the occupations and marched in the demonstrations; some have lent space to the movement, made financial donations, given food. While we have no real evidence, it's hard to imagine that the Occupy movement isn't having an impact on workers' consciousness. As with the civil rights movement of the 1960s which after the long dark night of McCarthyism once again legitimated protest, so too Occupy today is legitimating social protest on the left. Once again it is okay to say that you don't like the system and disagree with the government. If the movement grows, it will become almost a moral obligation to be a dissenter.

Occupy Wall Street and Politics

Occupy, of course, preoccupies the politicians. The Republican Party, naturally, loathes the politics of Occupy. House Majority leader Eric Cantor referred to the Occupiers as "mobs." Alluding to President Barack Obama he said, "Some in this town condone pitting Americans against Americans." Mitt Romney, the leading contender for the Republican presidential nomination said, "I think it's dangerous, this class warfare." Whatever they may say to the media, the Republicans' real fear is that Occupy Wall Street could buoy up the Democrats, while their hope that the movement's radicalism will blow their opponents to the left, costing them votes in the center. No doubt the Republicans sense the radical character of the movement and fear it.

One of the impacts of Occupy is that it has displaced the Tea Party, at least for now. Where just a few months ago the Tea Party dominated the news, now it is Occupy Wall Street that captures the headlines and the imagination of the public. While the Tea Party had already gone into decline before Occupy emerged, it has now all but disappeared from the media and the public mind. A CBS/*New York Times* poll conducted in late October found that 43 percent of the population agrees with the Occupy Wall Street movement. At the same time, a Congressional Budget Office study confirmed Occupy's claim that the 1 percent was enriching itself at the expense of the 99 percent.

The Democratic Party Congressional Campaign Committee and the think-tank Center for American Program are trying to find a way to use Occupy Wall Street, believing that the movement could put wind in the party's sails for 2012. Other party leaders fear that the identification with the movement would move the party toward the left and away from the center where they believe the voters are. Even more important, some Democratic Party leaders sense that opposing Wall Street implicitly challenges the whole *raison d'être* of the Democrats as a party that binds the middle class, the working class and the poor to the corporate order. And more practically speaking, some Democratic Party leaders have argued that such an attack on Wall Street could result in fewer donations from the banks and corporations that fund the Democrats. Bernie Sanders, the only independent in the Senate who calls himself a socialist (though he caucuses with the Democrats) spoke to the Occupy movement with an op-ed piece calling upon the government to break up the banks, support small business, and stop speculation in the oil industry. That was the Progressive Party program of 1912, the traditional program of American populism, but it misses completely the radical spirit of this movement.

Some Democrats would like to see Occupy Wall Street become their Tea Party, the right wing group that brought new vitality to the Republicans. But Occupy Wall Street activists have kept their distance from the Democrats, generally declining to provide a platform for the politicians or party candidates. At the moment there seems little chance of this as the Occupy movement jealously guards its independence.

Once again, after forty years of relative political and social stagnation, we have a mass movement with a radicalizing tendency. It faces the common problem of such suddenly emerging movements, that there are not enough leaders, that there is not enough organization, there is not enough yet of a strongly held radical political ideology. The notion of the "99 percent" and the idea that "We are what democracy looks like" and declaration of the Occupy Wall Street movement are good starting points. Still, we need to have a clearer notion of what we stand for in this movement. This is not a call for a political program or a formal set of demands. At present, the movement draws its strength precisely from its moral rejection of the system and projection that another sort of society, another world is possible.

Our job on the left is to work with others on the left and in the various social movements as well as within Occupy to help develop the leadership, organizational strength, and clear ideology that can both help to take Occupy forward toward the assertion of political independence, beyond the confining structures of the Republican and Democratic parties, so that down the road the movement can stimulate the birth of a party that actually represents the radical aspiration of the occupiers in the face of the coming crises and the even more expansive upheavals that lie ahead.

9

Lessons Learned from the Occupy Movement

Eric Westervelt

Eric Westervelt is an award-winning journalist who helped launch the National Public Radio platform "NPR Ed." He has covered politics and public affairs both in America and around the world, including Berlin, Baghdad, and Israel.

In this viewpoint, NPR's Eric Westervelt interviews Micah White, a founding member of the Occupy Wall Street protests in 2011, about his experiences with the Occupy movement and what those experiences taught him about the strategy of protest in contemporary America. While White is opposed to the content of President Trump's political beliefs and actions, he considers his status as a political outsider who managed to reach the masses as a sign of the possibility of political change and anti-establishmentarianism in the future.

D isillusioned with traditional protest, activist, writer and Occupy Wall Street co-creator Micah White moved to rural Nehalem, Ore.—population 280—not long after the Occupy movement fizzled out to run for local office and test out an idea of social change.

"We could have activists take over small towns for the benefit of people who live there and the people who are going to move there, and actualize all of the grand ideas that we have on the left," he tells me. "That's where I'm at as an activist, thinking, 'Is that possible?'"

I reported from Nehalem and toured the town with him. I also interviewed White at length at his home there. Here's that conversation, edited for length and clarity.

You've gone from trying to look at the big picture, global "We are the 99 percent," stop the money in politics, end corporate greed down to 280 people. Why go small?

I think one of the things about being an activist is what you have to do is you have to first create a theory of social change and then also you have to test it out. Occupy Wall Street tested out a grand theory of social change, which was basically, "If you can get millions of people into the streets, largely non-violent, and unified behind a central message, then change will have to happen." I think we spread to 82 countries. It was amazing. And it didn't work.

In that constructive failure I re-assessed and I was like, "You know, I think the reason it didn't work was because there's something fundamentally broken about protest." I ended up moving to small town Oregon and realizing, "Here's another theory of how social change could happen."

There's certainly debate about Occupy's overall impact, but ultimately, both in your book (*The End Of Protest: A New Playbook For Revolution*) and in your talks, you seem to come down pretty firmly on one side of that debate, as someone who helped co-found it and get it started. You see it as a failure.

This is the fundamental thing. I think one of the problems with contemporary activism is that we've really lowered our horizon of possibility. We've really changed what we think success is. If you look at the 18th, 19th, 20th centuries, what did success mean as a political activist, a political revolutionary? It meant the Russian revolution, the Chinese revolution, or the American Revolution. Taking control of one's government, changing the way power functions.

Success now has become something like getting a lot of people to hear about my meme. Or changing the discourse. We changed the discourse. We trained a whole new generation of activists, but we didn't change how power functions. That's what our real goal was. I think that's an indictment of contemporary activism. We spread to 82 countries faster than any social movement has ever spread that fast. And it didn't work. I think it's really important as an activist to constantly learn from one's past failures. I think a lot of activists don't want to learn from Occupy Wall Street.

When I look at activism in the six years since Occupy, they're repeating the same mistake over and over and over again. We have become obsessed with the spectacle of street protests, and we have started to ignore the reality that we are getting no closer to power. You would think that with the triumph of Trump there would be a fundamental reassessment among activists. But there hasn't been. They've just doubled down on the same behaviors!

Right. When you say it was a constructive failure, it's constructive only if people learn from it. You're saying, in the age of Trump, there is a kind of fetishization of street protest and spectacle over substance?

Yeah, we've come to a dangerous point where what's really going on, and this is the deep thing that no one wants to talk about, which is that the left has been taken over by anti-revolutionaries. The left actually doesn't really believe in the desirability or possibility of revolution anymore. I think that has a lot to do with the trauma of our past revolutions: the experience of the cultural revolution in China, the Stalinist gulags. All of that kind of stuff has turned the left into people who believe in reform, not revolution.

Now look at the right. The right's all about revolution worldwide. That's why they're winning. I think that's really the fundamental problem here. People who celebrate the grand successes of Black Lives Matter and Occupy and Standing Rock and all these protests. It feels really good to celebrate those things as success, but it's leading us further and further away from real success, and that's dangerous. I mean we're seeing how dangerous that is right now with Trump in so many ways. He is fundamentally pushing our world into a dark place. So it's very dangerous for the left to continue to treat online social marketing as if it were social activism. Protest alone does not give us political power. That's why we have Trump right now.

But an activist who's been in the cold at Standing Rock, or out in the street for Black Lives Matter, or who was at one the many Occupy protests might say, "Micah's sitting in Nehalem, Ore., population 280, telling me the best way to protest? He needs to walk the walk." What are you really doing to walk the walk here in your community?

I've been an activist since I was 13, so my whole life has been doing this. I think it's very possible for us to build a social movement that would win elections in many, many rural communities very quickly. Much more quickly than anyone's ever seen. I think that it is conceivable that we could wake up and we could have activists controlling literally the local level in a way that we've never seen before. With that power, we'd have the sovereignty to pass legislation that really fundamentally affects people's lives.

In Nehalem, Ore., where I live, we have a $700,000 budget surplus [Note: the city manager calls it an emergency fund] because of all the timber land that we own. If there were activists who controlled city council, it would be very easy for us to say that no child shall be hungry within our community. Or we could say, "Every child shall have college grants" if they want that. Or student loan forgiveness. Or whatever. Basically all of these ideas that have been floating around within activist communities, we could actually carry them out quite simply. I look at it and I just see that we've become very good at getting millions of people into the streets and we're very bad at winning elections.

You ran for city office. Tell us how that worked out?

Yeah. I ran for mayor (in November). It was probably one of the most fascinating experiences in my life and it was a huge growing experience for me. Nehalem's a microcosm. The reason why I lost the election I think is so much tied in to what's going on nationally and globally right now. First of all, just to give people a sense of what happened, I got 20 percent of the vote which I think is actually pretty amazing as someone who's a black American in rural white Oregon speaking about revolution. I wrote a book with revolution in the title, I'm a former Occupy guy. Still, one out of five people voted for me.

The basic platform wasn't vote for Micah White. It was instead this idea of, "Let's create something called a Nehalem's People's Associations and before each city council meeting let's go to those people's associations, let's get together with our neighbors and let's talk about what city council should do the following day. Let's move power away from city council to these Nehalem People's Associations." I told people, "If I'm elected mayor, then I will basically abide by the decisions of the people who come to these meetings." I had five of them before each city council meeting over the course of five months. There were so many people who showed up. We passionately debated things. People were on both sides—against and for. It was like the first time, I think, that people from across the political spectrum who live in this tiny town sat in the same room together and debated things like, "Change is happening in our community. How do we navigate it? What do we want it to look like in the future?" and all this kind of stuff. It was really beautiful.

What did the opposition do? It's the same thing that happened on the national level. All of a sudden I was hit with fake news. All of a sudden there's these rumors going around. People started asking me, "Are you a satanist?" I was like, "Whoa. First of all, what is even a satanist?" People literally believed I'm doing Satan worshiping exercises somewhere. I had no idea how to respond to that. It was like Pizzagate, if people remember that. All of sudden people were convinced that there was a child pedophilia ring in the basement of a pizza place in D.C. It's like that. They were just convinced I was a satanist!

Wait. Satanist. How did the satanist charge start? Did you say something that got twisted, or no?

Someone in Portland decided that they were going to try [to] start satanist clubs at elementary schools in Oregon. They just by chance happened to pick Nehalem Elementary School, which is a few blocks from my house. So a disconnected event, someone tried to start a satanist club. Other event—Micah's running for mayor. There must be some sort of connection here!

So people were like, Micah White, he's an after school satanist?

Exactly. And meanwhile I don't have a child at the elementary school. I'm not a satanist. I don't believe in Satan. I'm against Satan. I actually love good. That's why I do social activism. I'm trying to create a better place. The thing about fake news is they don't ask you. They don't ask you.

So this activist from Berkeley and Occupy comes out here to a small town saying we need a local revolution? Talk about the kind of pushback you got besides the satanist charge.

That's what I think is so interesting again about the Nehalem experience and I think why solving how to win elections in rural communities will actually unlock a global challenge. People actually started a counter-campaign against me called, "Keep Nehalem Nehalem." Basically that summarizes what it was about, which was basically, "We don't want change. Keep it the way it is." They wanted to say that I was the driver of change, when instead I was saying, "Change is happening in this community. The demographics are changing already. I'm a symptom of that but there's other people here—the 20 percent who voted for me—who are also symptomatic of that. Let's figure out how to navigate the change."

I feel like it's the forces who can navigate change who will win right now. The forces like Trump who just want to say, "Let's close our borders. We don't need to figure out about climate change. We don't need to figure out about immigration or understand why (refugees) are having to move here." They're the ones who are ultimately going to lose.

Well you say "they're ultimately going to lose." But there's these right-wing populist nationalist movements in the US and across many countries, especially Europe—Netherlands, Hungary, Poland—saying, "This change is really scary. I'll help you navigate it." What do you say to a Steve Bannon or others who might say, "You still don't get why Donald Trump is president. He attracted working-class folks who were fed up with elites trying to spoon-feed them their solution"?

I think the best example is climate change. Donald Trump doesn't have a plan for solving climate change because it would require a global response. He doesn't believe in global responses, so he denies that it exists.

Ultimately they can't solve the thing that really needs solving. Because of that, I think that we're going to swing back into power. We need a global populism. We need another vision of globalism. That's what's really at stake here, is two visions of populism. One, charismatic single individuals like Donald Trump and Putin. Another, social movements that can win elections in multiple countries, things like Podemos in Spain, the Five Star Movement in Italy, the Pirate Party in Iceland. These are competing visions for how power should function, and I think our vision is ultimately better—if we can figure it out.

Do you think the Democratic Party could ever be a vehicle for real transformation, or in your view is the party too tainted by money to ever be able to become a viable progressive vehicle again?

I'm much, much more tantalized by the possibility of a new social movement. A new political party that can sweep America and also other countries too. I think the Democratic Party, these establishment types, they're so desperate to co-opt social protests back into getting themselves into power that ultimately I think they're very, very detrimental to our success. I'm not into the

Bernie Sanders, Elizabeth Warren, Democratic Party resurgence stuff. I think that those people will constantly pull us back into a vision of globalism that seriously is broken. They're not challenging the way power functions. They're not saying, "Let's use Internet voting." They're not putting forward any different way for how power should function. They're just basically saying, "I'm a better person, so I should be in power."

What's fundamentally wrong about Donald Trump isn't whether or not he's a good or bad person. It's about how he thinks power should function, which is autocratically.

President Trump has explicitly stated an anti-globalist view. He has said, basically, "I'm not president of the world. I don't salute some world flag. I'm president of the United States and it's America first."

That's the deep irony and every time I end up talking about Donald Trump I give him some weird underhanded compliments. What he really represents is he's the shadow of Occupy Wall Street. He's the shadow of the anti-globalization movement. He basically is the "get-money-out-of-politics" candidate. He won the election by spending half as much as Hillary Clinton. We thought that wasn't possible. Look, he did it. He's anti-globalization. He's the negative shadow of the positive vision that we were trying to put forward.

You're giving Donald Trump a kind of grudging hat tip. He's an outsider who harnessed populist power to win an election. He didn't spend a lot on advertising. He held rallies. He mobilized ordinary people and they won real power.

Yeah, Donald Trump proves that it's possible for an outsider to win elections in America. So I celebrate him for that. I love his spirit. I love things that he said during the debates. I love his anti-establishmentism. I love that he says things like, before the election he said, "If I don't win the primary there's going to be riots in the streets." I love that. And I love Steve Bannon's Leninist spirit. I love all that stuff. Ultimately what's wrong with it is that they are ill-equipped to deal with the actual challenges that we face. They're scapegoating the weakest people in our community in order to not solve the real challenges like economic and environmental problems.

When you look at people planning things like the March for Science coming up in April and other planned marches and protests, what would be your message to them?

I think that my message to activists today is—never protest the same way twice. Social protest seems to work most effectively when the tactics that we use are new. I think that as activists, we have a tendency instead to do the opposite. We have the tendency to repeat. If you look at Occupy Wall Street, it started as Occupy Wall Street, and then it became Occupy London, and then it became Occupy Sandy, like we occupied a storm. Basically everything becomes Occupy. Every time you repeat a tactic it becomes less effective. So if you're going to use traditional social protest, at least, at the very least vary your tactics such that it's always a surprise.

When you look at the history of direct action protests, sometimes smaller change-it-up groups, like ACT UP, arguably had a bigger impact overall than some of the big anti-war marches.

We do live in a time of increasing frequency and size of social protests. But that does not mean that these social protests are becoming more effective.

You can get 4 million people into the streets and there is no requirement in our Constitution or in our laws that the president has to listen. He's able to say, "Thanks, go home now." And they go home. We need to stop with this naïve belief that if we just get more people into the streets, then we'll get what we want. No, it's not true! They don't have to listen anymore.

10

The Modern Face of White Nationalism in America

Andrew Gumbel

Andrew Gumbel is a British journalist and writer. He has worked as a foreign correspondent for the Guardian *in Europe as well as in the United States and the Middle East.*

In this viewpoint, Andrew Gumbel examines the peculiar ability of white nationalist protestors to evade conviction in US courts, even when their actions are illegal in a relatively straightforward sense. He suggests that US jurors are more sympathetic to right-wing political agitators than they are to most defendants, which helps them to evade conviction. As a result, the residing anti-establishment anger in America has hindered rule of law.

Conventional wisdom has it that defendants never catch a break in US federal court: the conviction rate last year was more than 95%. But it seems those odds improve if, like the leaders of last winter's armed standoff at the Malheur National Wildlife Refuge in Oregon, you are part of the radical anti-government right.

The decision by a Portland jury to acquit the Bundy brothers, Ammon and Ryan, and five others on conspiracy and firearms charges on Thursday night marks the third time in 28 years that

"How the Oregon Militia Acquittals Reflect the Appeal of White Nationalist Agitators," by Andrew Gumbel, Guardian News and Media Limited, October 29, 2016. Reprinted by permission.

a high-profile federal case involving armed anti-government agitators has collapsed.

In each case, questions have arisen over whether white nationalist agitators evoked sympathies among jurors that other defendants do not.

Four years ago, an attempt to charge members of the Hutaree Christian militia in Michigan with sedition ended in similar embarrassment for the government after the judge said there was no evidence the five defendants intended to attack anyone, much less murder a police officer and ambush his funeral as the prosecution alleged.

In 1988, another sedition trial in Fort Smith, Arkansas—this one featuring a rogue's gallery of more than a dozen of America's most visible far-right anti-government luminaries, some of them already serving long sentences for violent crimes—also led to acquittals all around, not to mention the marriage of a juror to one of the defendants.

In the wake of the Portland verdict, some civil rights advocates and anti-gun activists were quick to suggest a double standard when it comes to civil disobedience and attitudes to gun ownership.

"Apparently it's legal in America for heavily armed white terrorists to invade Oregon," the former TV talk show host Montel Williams wrote on Twitter. "Imagine if some black folk did this."

On the other side of the political fence, some suggested the prosecutors may simply have overreached. Sedition is notoriously hard to prove and the charge has been leveled only a handful of times since the founding of the republic for that reason. In the Oregon case, one juror said he would have had no problem convicting the defendants of trespassing but the conspiracy charge, which carries much stiffer penalties, was a stretch.

In an age of anti-establishment anger, jurors also appear to have been swayed by the sheer confidence of the prosecuting attorneys.

"The air of triumphalism that the prosecution brought was not lost on any of us," juror four wrote to the *Oregonian* newspaper, "nor was it warranted given their burden of proof."

Mark Pitcavage of the Anti-Defamation League, one of America's foremost authorities on rightwing extremism, said he could only imagine that courtroom dynamics along these lines had undone what had otherwise seemed like a very strong government case.

"I was hardly alone in thinking that," he said. "The mere fact that many of the standoff defendants entered into plea deals rather than go to trial suggests that they and their attorneys also felt the government had a very strong case."

There was similar incredulity at the not guilty verdicts in Fort Smith in 1988, as analysts pondered how the government could possibly lose a case against leaders and foot soldiers of the Ku Klux Klan and Aryan Nations, among other organizations, some of whom had previously been proven to have robbed banks and armored trucks, killed people, and openly called for the violent overthrow of the government.

On that occasion, the jury's sympathy for the defendants was clear. One female juror started up a romance with defendant David Lane, previously convicted of murdering a talk-radio host in Denver. Another female juror ended up marrying David McGuire, charged with plotting to kill an FBI agent and a federal judge.

It didn't help that the judge dispensed with standard jury selection and hand-picked an all-white panel over the objections of the prosecution.

"If we'd had good jury selection, I think we would have won the case," the FBI agent targeted for assassination, Jack Knox, said in an interview years later. "The judge … was dredging right at the bottom of the barrel."

Another former FBI agent with extensive experience of the radical far right, Danny Coulson, did not exclude the possibility of similar sympathies being at play in the Oregon case—on the side of law enforcement as much as the jury. Portland may be a liberal city, he said, but gun culture is deeply entrenched in Oregon and many people may have had some bedrock sympathy for the protesters' complaints.

"It's the tenor of the times," Coulson said in an interview. "A lot of people in our country are sick of government trying to control every aspect of human life.

"I'm not saying I agree with that position, but there are a lot of people who make that case … The bureau [FBI] is brought into this stuff all the time, and they don't want to do it. They don't want to be brought into it, and they probably have some sympathy for the cause."

Pitcavage did not agree that sympathy for far-right defendants was a given, in this or any other case.

"Almost every prosecution of rightwing extremism is successful," he said. "Our prisons are full of rightwing extremists. It's no more difficult to prosecute rightwing extremists than any other class of people. With any particular trial, though, there can be things that affect it."

11

Black Lives Matter and the Path from Protest to Policy

Jamilah King

Jamilah King is a New York-based writer focused on issues involving race, gender, and culture. She formerly served as senior editor at the journal Colorlines.

In this viewpoint, Jamilah King looks at the Black Lives Matter movement as well as other contemporary protests in the United States. She focuses on issues related to mobilizing outrage and protest toward legislative and policy action. She asserts that Black Lives Matter differs from other political movements in its refusal to endorse establishment politicians and policies, but while the movement has been accused of being disorganized and without clear goals, it has laid out its core demands and specific policy suggestions. It is also credited with helping more people of color and women get elected to local political office.

What role should identity play in our fight for freedom? After the election of Donald Trump as president of the US, the answer for many mainstream pundits has been simple: none. Particularly disheartening since the 2016 election has been the misguided view that black activism and its focus on racial justice, police accountability and—gasp—reparations for chattel slavery and decades of housing discrimination, was ultimately a divisive distraction from the larger goal of keeping a man who is sympathetic to white nationalists out of the Oval Office.

Depending on who you ask, black people shortchanged democracy either directly, by refusing to use their platform to endorse candidates, or indirectly by not voting with the same enthusiasm that ushered Barack Obama into the White House. The day after the election, *US News & World Reports* ran a story that summed this up: "Clinton made her case to black voters," the headline screamed. "Why didn't they hear her?"

This blame is neither new nor particularly compelling. Alicia Garza, a co-founder of the Movement for Black Lives coalition, Black Lives Matter and longtime organizer in black and Latino communities, sees it as part of a long history of wrongly blaming black people for the fundamental failings of electoral politics. "There's a contradiction happening where now white liberals and white moderates are saying, 'Man, we lost the election because black people didn't vote, so f--k BLM,' and 'We lost the election because we spent too much time on identity politics, but let's do everything we can to galvanize white working class people.'"

There has been a not-so-subtle insistence across US media and politics that white working-class voters have been ignored for the sake of radical rabble-rousers calling for justice based on who they love, their gender identity, their class background, and their racial identity. At its core is the belief that whiteness is and should remain the norm and that white supremacy is an immoveable and non-threatening platform on which to advocate for incremental change. The Movement for Black Lives has long argued that this is not a feasible road to freedom.

More Than a Hashtag

Black Lives Matter is a history that is still being written. Garza, Patrisse Khan-Cullors and Opal Tometi turned their collective outrage into action upon George Zimmerman's acquittal after killing Trayvon Martin in July 2013.

Garza, Khan-Cullors and Tometi were also among the protesters and organizers who flooded Ferguson, Missouri, for weeks after Michael Brown was shot dead by Darren Wilson, a white police officer in August 2014. Brown's body was left in the hot Missouri sun for hours.

The immediate shock of Brown's death gave way to a sobering look at the institutional forces that shape the lives and deaths of black people in places like Ferguson. The Department of Justice eventually issued a scathing report that detailed how Ferguson's courts and police force strategically targeted black citizens for arrest and fines to add millions of dollars to the city's coffers.

Meanwhile, organizers around the country joined Garza, Khan-Cullors and Tometi to turn #BlackLivesMatter into more than a hashtag. They created the Black Lives Matter Network and the Movement for Black Lives, the latter a coalition that included the Network and over 50 other racial justice organizations.

In April 2016, shortly after the Republican and Democratic Conventions, the Movement for Black Lives unveiled a long-awaited policy platform that outlined its essential beliefs. It laid out six core demands and 40 corresponding policy recommendations, including a call to demilitarize law enforcement, end money bail and end the privatization of public grammar school education in the US. The platform was bold not just in its recommendations, but also in its process. Officially titled "Vision for Black Lives: Policy Demands for Black Power, Freedom and Justice," the platform was the result of a year's work by the coalition. It was proof that there is a vast, co-ordinated movement in the US that is determined to fight for black freedom.

But it was also proof that that movement is fragmented. One of the more contentious splits has been between Movement for Black Lives co-founders and another group called We The Protesters, led by high-profile activist DeRay McKesson. A charter school educator by training, McKesson rose to prominence during the uprising in Ferguson where he live-tweeted on-the-ground events, gave interviews on cable news and amassed hundreds of thousands of followers, including Beyoncé.

A Challenge to Power

Many of the differences between the two groups can be boiled down to ideology. More often than not, the Movement for Black Lives has eschewed attempts to work within law enforcement or electoral politics, arguing that policy reform is only one tactic in an arsenal with plenty of others; We The Protesters, on the other hand, has zeroed in on pragmatic policy solutions and welcomed the chance to work with elected officials, such as accepting invitations to meet with Senator Bernie Sanders and Hillary Clinton during the 2016 election. They released their own policy platform focused specifically on police use of force.

The Movement for Black Lives has spurned advances from establishment politicians. They refused to fall in line with the status quo and disrupted liberal and progressive presidential candidates like Clinton and Sanders at rallies and fundraisers. They did not stop at calling for an end to the extrajudicial killings of black men and boys like Trayvon Martin and Michael Brown. Instead, they also demanded that the public at large, particularly black communities, also acknowledge the epidemic of violence aimed at transgender women of colour, who are murdered at stunningly disproportionate rates in the US. Organizers like Elle Hearns, based in Cleveland, helped develop a political platform that made these lives and deaths pivotal to black liberation at large.

"In my work I've always tried to consider and understand the multitude of experiences that shape who I am as a black person and the experiences of those in my community," says Hearns, who has since co-founded the Marsha P Johnson Institute, named after the slain transgender icon who helped spark the 1969 Stonewall Rebellion. "Why it is important to always maintain space for sexuality and gender is because that's who we are." Garza and Khan-Cullors, who both identify as queer, used their increasingly public platforms to demand that race, sexual identity and gender be acknowledged as interwoven forces. In an early herstory of the movement published on *The Feminist Wire* in 2014, Garza put it this way: "Progressive movements in the United States have made some unfortunate errors when they push for unity at the expense of really understanding the concrete differences in context, experience and oppression," she wrote. "In other words, some want unity without struggle."

Today, that struggle continues on all fronts. The US is one of many countries that is witnessing the rise of white nationalist movements—identity politics, though it isn't often called as such. At a local level, women and people of colour are using their identities to springboard themselves into elected office and challenge the agendas that threaten their existence. And Black Lives Matter is still organizing and protesting in a city near you.

12

The Tea Party and Conservative Outrage in the United States

William H. Westermeyer

A cultural anthropologist whose research focuses on social movements and their impact on politics, William H. Westermeyer is an assistant professor of anthropology at High Point University.

In this viewpoint, William Westermeyer looks at the roots of the Tea Party movement in America, which appeared in 2009 in response to President Obama's election and the legislative push to enact the Affordable Care Act. He asserts that the movement was particularly effective because of its focus on local Tea Party groups and candidates. Through focusing their attention on local issues, Tea Party groups were more effective at disrupting the political climate and sowing discord.

In the first few months of President Barack Obama's administration in 2009, a new conservative, populist social movement burst onto the American political scene. Throughout the 2008 presidential campaign, conservative media had consistently stoked fears about Obama. After he took office, as a clearer picture emerged regarding the new president's policies on government spending and debt, a large group of conservative Americans nationwide—encouraged by conservative media—coalesced into a vibrant, unique, and effective movement called the Tea Party.

"How the Tea Party Transformed American Politics," by William H. Westermeyer, Sapiens, February 17, 2017. Reprinted by permission.

Among pundits and scholars, there was disagreement regarding what the politically fundamentalist Tea Party actually was. Was it the result of machinations by billionaire industrialists Charles and David Koch? Was it constructed from the compelling rhetoric of Fox News and syndicated talk show hosts like Glenn Beck and Rush Limbaugh? Or was it a spontaneous eruption by everyday people? Simply put, the Tea Party was—and is—all three.

Since the beginning, the Tea Party movement has been a network in which those three components—elite organizations, conservative media, and local groups of everyday citizens—are connected through social and mass media as well as interpersonal ties. This structure became apparent to me when I spent 18 months in 2010 and 2011 conducting ethnographic research with local groups of Tea Party activists in central North Carolina.

One of my fieldwork sites was a small picturesque town in the foothills of the Appalachian Mountains. Dixon,* North Carolina, is popular with tourists for its downtown that seems frozen in the 1950s. Formerly anchored by textile manufacturing and tobacco cultivation, the local economy had already been faltering for some time when the decline was accelerated by the passage of free-trade agreements in the 1990s and the end of tobacco price supports and quotas in 2004. After these economic assaults, many people were forced to seek employment elsewhere and now typically commute to larger cities in the Carolina Piedmont such as Winston-Salem, which is some 30 miles away.

In the summer of 2011, I attended a meeting of Dixon's city council. The cities and counties of the western Piedmont were forming a regional transportation authority, or consortium, to address their changing transportation needs, and the group wanted to recruit Dixon as a member. The question of the city's participation was to be the main topic at the city council meeting.

Dixon also contained a small but active local Tea Party group—the Adams County Tea Party*—which regarded regional transportation planning as an ominous and sinister plot to undermine their freedom. They—in accord with many Tea Partyists around the nation—viewed local land-use management, regional planning, and sustainable development as efforts guided by a set of United Nations regulations called Agenda 21.

Agenda 21, an action plan that emerged from the 1992 UN Conference on Environment and Development (or Earth Summit), offers voluntary sustainable-development guidelines for governments at the local and national levels. By 2011, Tea Party members around the nation were familiar with Agenda 21 because Tea Partyists had been circulating warnings about it through social media since 2009. They saw Agenda 21 as a plot by which transnational organizations were attempting to undermine the autonomy of local, regional, and national governments. According to Tea Partyists, such schemes would change their communities by mandating dense housing, limiting automobile use, and imposing social equity, as defined by Agenda 21. Social equity was seen as being dangerously similar to social justice, which—thanks to Tea Party prophet Glenn Beck— came to imply tyrannical social engineering.

Because Dixon's city council had invited a representative of the nascent regional transportation authority to brief the public on the plan that summer evening in 2011, Adams County Tea Party members saw Agenda 21 and its strategy for social equity coming to their picturesque little town. During the question-and-answer period after the presentation, the mild-mannered representative was peppered with questions about consolidated housing, the loss of local autonomy, and social engineering, resulting in exchanges like this:

> *Council member and Tea Party ally: Can you explain the social equity component?*
>
> *Consortium representative: Right now we have 1,600,000 people in the region. We will grow to about 2 million, so says the state demographer. We have a diverse population already. We have new immigrants and people who've been here for a long time. We have disparities within the region … [O]ne of our strengths—diversity … people working together on common problems will be a better place to be.*

Council member: So it really is social engineering.
Representative: I wouldn't call it that.
Tea party member: But that is what you just said.
Representative: I wouldn't call it that.

The representative told me later that many of the questions that Tea Party attendees threw at him were unfamiliar to him and seemed to misconstrue the plan. Crucially, he was unfamiliar with the specific meanings Tea Partyists attached to issues of regional planning and sustainable development. It was as if he and the Tea Partyists were discussing two entirely different plans, and he was left to offer responses like, "That is not planned by the consortium," and "I'm not aware of that restriction," which the Tea Partyists interpreted as evasive or untrue.

As a result, the city council was even more divided than before the meeting, and Adams County Tea Party members were able to call their efforts a "victory" on social media, thereby encouraging other Tea Party groups to engage in similar actions. Nearly six years later, Dixon is not a member of the consortium, and local governments across the nation have experienced protests against plans that were supposedly inspired by Agenda 21.

This scene illustrates a crucial, but not often discussed, factor in the Tea Party movement's success. Local activists were overlooked in many of the early accounts of the Tea Party, yet the groups I observed made local politics a primary site of conflict. It is important to stress that these local groups—then and still today—do not just form ad hoc for one event. Local Tea Party groups of 50 to 500 people regularly meet to learn about issues, exchange information, and report on and plan activities. In the process, these interactive social spaces provide the setting for Tea Party supporters to fashion durable identities as Tea Party activists. These newly minted activists are eager and willing to bring their beliefs in smaller government, lower taxes, and personal liberty into local political arenas, where they often have significant, while less-noticed, effects on important issues such as land use, city and regional planning, property taxes, and public education.

The Tea Party's success is to a large degree based on the socially constructed cultural world the movement has created, which forms the context for forging a powerful political identity. Simply put, the Tea Party network and its local participants create what it means to be a Tea Party member, an identity that entails a unique constellation of beliefs, practices, interpretive frames, and symbols.

The cultural world of the Tea Party contains three broad themes: patriotism and history, such as their emulation of the Founding Fathers; political and cultural fundamentalism, epitomized in their strict, literal interpretation of the United States Constitution and their resistance to compromise; and emotional registers of indignation and mistrust. Their identity is grounded in their sense of anger and loss with regard to values that they say made America exceptional—independence, self-reliance, and achievement. According to Tea Partyists, those values, espoused by the founders, enshrined in the Constitution, and held dear by previous generations, are being betrayed by the government's ever-expanding role and forsaken by most Americans.

The importance of local Tea Party groups becomes apparent when considered in this context. These groups meet regularly in secluded spaces where the Tea Party identity can be performed, strengthened, disclosed, and imparted to others. A crucial aspect of the Tea Party is outward political activism. The gatherings I studied were essentially workshops in democratic citizenship in which people learned and taught others to do activism, such as organizing protests and rallies, setting up phone trees to speak out on important legislation, testifying at public hearings, and conducting the myriad of activities involved in political campaigns.

Of the eight groups I observed, seven of them became effective local political actors. Two groups seized control of their county's Republican Party organizations. Another wrote a symbolic alternative budget for their county government that eliminated the need for a tax increase. All provided an army of get-out-the-vote ground troops who contributed to the massive GOP election victories that came out of the "Tea Party wave" in 2010. Tea Partyists and their newly elected allies helped block President Obama's agenda by presenting an uncompromising, indignant activism that influenced officeholders, media, and everyday citizens.

The local Tea Party groups I studied contextualized and acted on widely circulating conservative discourses in their own local arenas and in their own ways with few or no resources—and little direction—from outside organizations. In an era in which social media and the internet are rightly seen as primary sites of political struggle, these groups illustrate the continued importance of local, face-to-face political organizations in the development of effective activism and purposeful political identities.

Most people make sense of social and economic change within the context of their everyday lives and identities, such as their jobs, their communities, and the values they share in those spaces. If they come to believe the quality of those things is declining or threatened, they may blame corporations (or capitalism in general) if they are liberals. Most conservatives, by contrast, tend to blame the government. In Tea Partyists' eyes, the government has abandoned the Founding Fathers, the Constitution, and the very identity of America by altering the values that underlie them—liberty, individualism, and community. For Tea Partyists and Donald Trump supporters alike, their activism is a reaction to what they see as an attack on the very essence of themselves.

But while Trump certainly benefited from the Tea Party vote (you would be hard-pressed to find a Tea Partyist who voted for Democratic presidential nominee Hillary Clinton), there are important differences between Trump's supporters and many people who identify with the Tea Party. For one thing, there is little evidence that President Trump commands an activist constituency with a consistent collective identity.

Most of my informants favored presidential candidates Ted Cruz or Ben Carson early on, and while they were eventually compelled to support Trump, they were not as excited about the results of the election as I had anticipated. Their explanations made a lot of sense, though, when considered in the context of how Tea

Partyists interpret people and events. Trump is a pragmatist, often capricious, and not a political fundamentalist. He will not base his policies on constitutional literalism and most likely will not guide his actions according to what George Washington or Benjamin Franklin would have done.

That said, anger toward a cultural and political elite above and the indolent "other" below—whether immigrants, public employees, or welfare recipients—is a common characteristic among both Trump supporters and Tea Partyists.

The Tea Party has been effective not because of mass demonstrations—though some of them were quite impressive—but due to localized, well-planned actions within institutional political arenas. In other words, their effects were felt in local and national legislative bodies and state-level party organizations—not in the streets. Attending a rally or protest is fun and salves one's sense of powerlessness, but it does not replace sustained, mundane organizing. Granted, the Tea Party's agenda was amplified by Fox News and other conservative media, but the activists' identities were forged in groups that met regularly—in some cases, every week—in secluded social spaces. Those spaces were used for workshops in democratic citizenship, where novice supporters learned political organizing skills from experienced Tea Partyists. Their activism was not episodic; it was routine.

The routine activism and the ideological consistency of the Tea Party are not, to my knowledge, qualities that are present to such a degree among Trump supporters. Though media personalities like Sean Hannity and Rush Limbaugh have been important to forging Trump's support, even Republican lawmakers have pointed out his lack of conservative ideology. In the breathtaking first weeks of Trump's presidency, questions about his relationship to the Tea Party, and about the depth and breadth of his support, have become more and more pressing: Over the coming months and years, will President Trump prove able to corral a loose coalition of support into a unified, effective movement? And if he does, will the Tea Party be part of that movement, or will it maintain its distinctive, cohesive identity—as the uncompromising defender of the Constitution and American exceptionalism—which has made it so effective in recent years?

No matter what happens, one thing is certain: We are entering uncharted political territory where new contours of social movements and American political culture are likely to be revealed.

To protect the privacy of my informants, I've used the fictitious names Dixon and Adams County Tea Party throughout this piece.

13

Weaponized Outrage: The Russian Campaign to Influence American Politics

Timothy Summers

Timothy Summers is a professor of innovation and entrepreneurship at the University of Maryland and the CEO of Summers & Company, a cyber strategy consultancy.

In this viewpoint, Timothy Summers examines the Russian plot to spread disinformation and inflammatory content among online networks of US voters ahead of the 2016 presidential election. He suggests that the inflammatory nature of political discourse on social media made US voters vulnerable to Russian trolls and their campaign of disinformation. The political polarization in the United States allowed Russian propaganda to be effective, with Russian trolls simply having to encourage further discord.

The Soviet Union and now Russia under Vladimir Putin have waged a political power struggle against the West for nearly a century. Spreading false and distorted information—called "dezinformatsiya" after the Russian word for "disinformation"—is an age-old strategy for coordinated and sustained influence campaigns that have interrupted the possibility of level-headed political discourse. Emerging reports that Russian hackers targeted a Democratic senator's

"How the Russian Government Used Disinformation and Cyber Warfare in 2016 Election—an Ethical Hacker Explains," by Timothy Summers, *The Conversation*, July 28, 2018. https://theconversation.com/how-the-russian-government-used-disinformation-and-cyber-warfare-in-2016-election-an-ethical-hacker-explains-99989. Licensed under CC BY-ND 4.0.

2018 reelection campaign suggest that what happened in the lead-up to the 2016 presidential election may be set to recur.

As an ethical hacker, security researcher and data analyst, I have seen firsthand how disinformation is becoming the new focus of cyberattacks. In a recent talk, I suggested that cyberwarfare is no longer just about the technical details of computer ports and protocols. Rather, disinformation and social media are rapidly becoming the best hacking tools. With social media, anyone—even Russian intelligence officers and professional trolls—can widely publish misleading content. As legendary hacker Kevin Mitnick put it, "it's easier to manipulate people rather than technology."

Two sets of federal indictments—one in February and another in July—allege in detail how a private company linked to Putin and the Russian military itself worked to polarize American political discourse and sway the 2016 U.S. presidential election.

Cybersecurity experts in the US knew that the Russian intelligence agencies were conducting these acts of information warfare and cyberwarfare, but I doubt they had any idea how comprehensive and integrated they were—until now.

Russia's Propaganda Machine Duped American Voters

The operation was complex. What is publicly known now is perhaps most easily understood in two pieces, the subjects of separate federal indictments.

First, a billionaire Russian businessman and Putin associate allegedly assembled a network of troll factories: private Russian companies engaging in a massive disinformation campaign. Their employees posed as Americans, created racially and politically divisive social media groups and pages, and developed fake news articles and commentary to build political animosity within the American public.

Second, the Russian military intelligence agency, known by its Russian acronym as the GRU, allegedly used coordinated hacking to target more than 500 people and institutions in the United States. The Russian hackers downloaded potentially damaging information and released it to the public via WikiLeaks and under various aliases including "DCLeaks" and "Guccifer 2.0."

Online Trolls Manipulated Your Opinions

The people involved did not fit the stereotypical picture of internet trolls. One leading Russian troll factory was a company called the Internet Research Agency, reportedly with all the trappings of a real corporation, including a graphics department to create incendiary images, a foreign department dedicated to following political discourse in other countries and an IT department to make sure trolls had reliable computers and internet connections. Employees, mostly 18 to 20 years old, were paid as much as US$2,100 a month for creating fake social media accounts and blogs to distribute disinformation to Americans.

They were employed to take advantage of deepening political polarization in the US. The Russians saw this as an opportunity to stir up conflict—like poking a stick into a beehive. These trolls were instructed to stir up racial tensions, stage "flash mobs" and organize activist campaigns—sometimes announcing events for opposing groups at the same times and locations.

One ex-troll told a Russian independent TV network that his job included writing incendiary comments and creating fake posts on political forums: "The way you chose to stir up the situation, whether it was commenting [on] the news section or on political forums, it didn't really matter." In 2015, well before the 2016 election, the troll-factory network had more than 800 people doing this kind of work, producing propaganda videos, infographics, memes, reports, news, interviews and various analytical materials to persuade the public.

America never stood a chance.

Focusing on Social Media

It's no surprise that these Russian trolls spent most of their time on Facebook and Instagram: Two-thirds of Americans get at least some news on social media. The trolls spread out across both platforms, seeking to encourage conflict on any topic that was getting a lot of attention: immigration, religion, the Black Lives Matter movement and other hot-button issues.

When describing how he managed all of the fake social media accounts, the ex-troll said: "First, you gotta be a redneck from Kentucky, then you need to be a white guy from Minnesota, you've slaved away all your life and paid your taxes, and then 15 minutes later you are from New York posting in some Black slang."

Then, the indictments reveal, the GRU entered this increasingly fraught online political discourse.

The GRU Weighs In

Like another significant political scandal, the GRU effort allegedly started with a break-in to Democratic National Committee records—but this time it was a digital burglary. It wasn't particularly sophisticated, either, using two common hacking techniques, spearphishing and malicious software.

As the July indictment details, starting in March 2016, Russian military operatives sent a series of fake emails, disguised to look real, to more than 300 people associated with Democratic National Committee, the Democratic Congressional Campaign Committee and Hillary Clinton's presidential campaign. One of the targets was Clinton campaign chairman John Podesta, who fell for the scheme and unwittingly handed over more than 50,000 emails to the Russians.

Around the same time, the Russian hackers allegedly began searching for technical vulnerabilities in the Democratic organizations' computer networks. They used techniques and specialized malicious software that Russians had used in other hacking efforts, including against the German Parliament and the French television network TV5 Monde. By April 2016, the hackers had gained access to the Democratic Congressional Campaign Committee systems, exploring servers and secretly extracting sensitive data. They located a Democratic Congressional Campaign Committee staffer who also had privileges in the Democratic

National Committee systems, and thereby got into the Democratic National Committee networks too, extracting more information.

When the Democratic National Committee realized there was unusual data traffic in its systems, the group hired a private cybersecurity firm, which in June 2016 publicly announced that its investigation had concluded that Russia was behind the hacking. At that point, the Russians allegedly tried to delete traces of their presence on the networks. But they kept all the data they had stolen.

Opposing Hillary Clinton

As early as April 2016, the GRU was allegedly trying to use the Democrats' confidential documents and email messages to stir up political trouble in the US. There is evidence that the Russian government, or people acting on its behalf, offered key people in the Trump campaign damaging information on Clinton.

In July 2016, the indictments say, the GRU began releasing many of the Democrats' documents and email messages, mainly through WikiLeaks, an internet site dedicated to anonymous publishing of secret information.

All of this effort was, according to the indictments, set up to undermine Hillary Clinton in the eyes of the American public. Putin definitely wanted Trump to win—as the Russian president himself acknowledged while standing next to Trump in Helsinki in July. And the trolls were instructed to go after her savagely: A former Russian troll said, "Everything about Hillary Clinton had to be negative and you really had to tear into her. It was all about the leaked email, the corruption scandals, and the fact that she is super rich."

The indictments describe in detail how information warfare and cyberwarfare were used as political tools to advance the interests of people in Russia. Something similar may be set to happen in 2018, too.

14

Protests, Policing, and the First Amendment

Mat dos Santos

Mat dos Santos serves as legal director for the American Civil Liberties Union of Oregon.

Mat dos Santos argues that excessive policing denies protestors the right guaranteed by the First Amendment to peacefully protest, as demonstrated by the use of police force on counter-protestors at a 2017 alt-right rally in Portland, Oregon. He asserts that the police are largely responsible for escalating violence at protests, and that in order to protect the constitutional right to publicly organize police must resort to crowd-control weapons as infrequently as possible.

O n Sunday, thousands of people peacefully assembled in downtown Portland to express themselves, just as the First Amendment envisions. A planned alt-right rally, the timing of which was awful and lacked respect for the city's grief over the murders on the MAX the previous week, drew many more counter-protesters than attendees. The tremendous outpouring of support from numerous immigrant rights groups, organized labor, faith based movements, and other antiracists showed the alt-right demonstrators that, while they have a constitutional right to speak, their message of white supremacy is unwelcome by the people of Portland.

"Sunday's Protests in Portland Were a Trial for the First Amendment and Policing," by Mat dos Santos, ACLU—American Civil Liberties Union of Oregon, June 6, 2017. Reprinted by permission.

This is the power of the First Amendment. When we organize and collectively raise our voices, we can reject the messages of hate and intolerance that permeate our communities.

For the first four hours of the demonstrations, law enforcement successfully kept groups separated in an effort to avoid conflict. Overall, the strategy of keeping people separated, while allowing each group to be heard, kept the peace for hours. Things took a dangerous turn as police deployed flashbang grenades, chemical irritants, and less-lethal bullets at the antifascist gathering—to the cheers of the alt-right group—after the police announced that projectiles and a foul-smelling liquid were thrown from the roof of the public bathroom in Chapman Park.

While we understand that policing is no easy task, the pattern in Portland is clear. After a rock, stick, or liquid is thrown, Portland protests regularly devolve into the indiscriminate use of force and crowd control weapons. Our democracy is not so fragile that a rock thrown turns off the First Amendment for everyone in our city. This kind of disproportionate response is dangerous to our democracy and our lives.

To our knowledge, no other police force in America uses crowd control weapons with the regularity of the Portland Police Bureau. It bears repeating that these "less lethal" weapons are dangerous and indiscriminate. In fact, our staff attorney, who was serving as legal observer in Chapman Square, was accosted with chemical irritants and then shot in the back of her leg as she was trying to comply with police orders. A street medic was shot while treating someone for injuries sustained during the police action. Flashbangs went off immediately behind an elderly person using a cane as they desperately tried to exit the park, causing her to stumble. These are just a few of many examples of innocent people being caught up in Sunday's police violence. It may be tempting to find comfort in the fact that in a very tense scenario things did not get far worse, but we cannot accept this as normal law enforcement behavior.

Unnecessary and excessive use of force isn't just bad for those caught up in the action, but it also stops members of the public from coming out and participating in our democracy. After police used crowd-control weapons on Sunday, many of the peaceful protesters gathered for a permitted counter-protest in front of City Hall left, fearful of being swept up in the police action. In other words, the actions of Portland law enforcement chilled the constitutionally-protected speech of peaceful protesters.

Unfortunately, the excessive response from law enforcement didn't stop at firing projectiles at Chapman Square. Police orders rapidly changed at this point and officers backed Chapman Square protesters all the way into Lownsdale Park, and then told them that it too was closed. Having been forced out of two public parks, protesters then began a spontaneous march through the streets. Police then blocked in or "kettled" everyone present on an entire city block where the spontaneous march was moving, nearly 200 people, and announced that they were detaining them to investigate disorderly conduct. Disorderly conduct is a minor offense and hardly something the police should prioritize at the expense of the constitutional rights of those who were detained.

Numerous members of the media and two ACLU legal observers were detained in that kettle. When they asked to be released, they were denied. It is unfathomable that the police had any basis for holding the media and ACLU legal observers for the purported investigation of particular subjects—the legal requirement for temporary detainment—of such a minor offense. Before allowing the protesters, bystanders, media, and legal observers to leave the kettle, law enforcement required each of them to show their ID, be photographed, and have their ID photographed. Some were told they could be arrested at a later day. The whole process took over an hour.

We have received many questions about the kettle, so let me take a minute to answer them:

1. Oregon law does not require people to show identification to the police, unless they are driving.

2. While police may detain someone suspected of committing a crime, they must actually be suspected of committing a

crime. It is virtually impossible that Portland Police had reasonable suspicion to stop nearly 200 people including media and legal observers.

3. Photographing the face and ID of every person detained is a likely violation of the Oregon state law prohibiting the collection and retention of personal information based on political beliefs.

4. If the information was subsequently entered into a federal database, Portland Police also likely violated federal privacy rules.

We are troubled by the continued crackdown on protest by Portland Police and cooperating agencies, but the kettling of individuals and refusal to let clearly innocent people free until they had been documented was another low for our city.

This weekend, Portland was a microcosm of all that is fundamental and also frightening about the First Amendment. It is sobering to hear the deeply traumatic and hurtful words of bigots. But on Sunday, we saw the resolute power of our fundamental freedoms of speech and assembly when we collectively came together to drown out bigotry.

15

The Impact of Mass Demonstrations on Policy

Alan Greenblatt

Alan Greenblatt is a staff writer at Governing *magazine. He previously covered politics for NPR and* CQ Weekly.

In this excerpted viewpoint, Alan Greenblatt connects the rise of public protests to President Donald Trump's election while also suggesting continuity with the widespread protests of the 1960s. He discusses the various types of protests and their efficacy by looking at historical examples in the United States. Ultimately, he suggests that protests are seldom effective at enacting specific policies, but they bring particular issues and alternative options to the public's awareness.

Dissent has always been part of American politics, but scholars say Donald Trump's election has sparked a heightened era of protests reflecting the country's deep ideological polarization. Fueled by social media, demonstrations have arisen over Trump administration policies on such issues as health care, climate change and immigration. Meanwhile, alleged police brutality and the removal of Confederate monuments have aroused mass protests, some violent. And on college campuses, students have clashed over whether right- and left-wing provocateurs should speak at public forums. In addition to using street protests, conservatives for decades have turned to ballot measures to oppose abortion,

"Do Mass Demonstrations Lead to Policy Changes?" Greenblatt, A. Citizen Protests. *CQ Researcher* 28(1), pp. 1-24. Copyright © 2018 by CQ Press. Reprinted by permission of SAGE Publications, Inc.

and more recently the tea party movement rallied against the Affordable Care Act and other policies championed by former President Barack Obama. But experts say the size and stridency of today's protests are reminiscent of the civil rights and anti-Vietnam War movements of the 1960s. Still, skeptics question whether street protests can change government policy, and some states are cracking down on protests that become disruptive or violent.

Overview

Like millions of Democrats, Anne Taussig was dismayed when Donald Trump was elected president. Unlike after past elections, however, she felt she could not wait four years before trying to do something about it.

The 66-year-old product designer from St. Louis opposes Trump's policies on issues such as taxes, health care and abortion and is concerned about his campaign's possible collusion with Russia. Thus, she became an activist in 2017, even though she had not participated in a street protest since college.

"We follow that strategy, to go after Trump the way the tea party went after [President] Obama," she says, referring to the conservative, antitax, populist movement that arose after the election of Barack Obama in 2008.

Taussig co-founded a St. Louis chapter of Indivisible, a left-leaning nationwide advocacy group that sprang up after Trump's election. Her chapter claims 3,000 members, many of whom routinely protest outside congressional offices or when administration officials come to town. The group showed up at the St. Louis airport last January, as activists did at other facilities around the country, to protest Trump's ban on travel from certain majority-Muslim countries.

Political protests are hardly new—citizens have demonstrated against government officials and policies they oppose since before the country was born. In recent years, conservatives held protests and disrupted town halls during Obama's presidency, complaining about deficit spending and health care policy. Anti-

Iraq War protests became routine during the George W. Bush administration.

But Trump's election has ushered in an era of heightened protest, according to those who study citizen activism. From marching and demonstrating to flooding Capitol Hill switchboards with phone calls, many Americans are voicing strident opposition to a president whose approval rating is consistently under 40 percent—historically low for a first-year president. At the same time, anti-Trump Americans are boycotting products associated with him or his family, while millions are expressing their anger on social media about his policies.

The question remains whether such protests matter: Trump has shown few signs of changing course on policy. Some, however, argue that the wave of popular dissent—dubbed by liberals as the "resistance"—has injected new life into liberal causes that will pay dividends in this year's midterm congressional elections and beyond.

"While Trump has given his followers the liberal tears they crave, that victory contains the seeds of its own reversal," wrote Michelle Goldberg, a *New York Times* opinion columnist.

Of course, it's not just liberals who embrace protests, and activism is not just about national politics. Conservatives have protested issues such as abortion, gay marriage, the growing national debt and the Affordable Care Act. Liberals have demanded action on climate change, environmental protection, LGBT rights and alleged police brutality against unarmed African-Americans. Angry protests also have erupted on college campuses in response to both liberal and conservative speakers. Native Americans and their allies have staged long-running protests against oil pipelines built on sacred Indian lands. And some white supremacists have taken to the streets to oppose the removal of Confederate monuments, among other causes.

In politics, such protests are part of an "outside game"—a strategy of agitating for or against policies from outside formal political institutions. The strategy can be part of an activist's toolkit for changing government or corporate practices, but some experts on activism say to effect change it must be followed up by long-term commitment to an "inside game"—lobbying and participation in political campaigns.

The tea party movement did just that. It started off holding large rallies, such as an antitax protest in Washington in 2009 that attracted as many as 70,000 people. Eventually, attending such protests largely gave way to organizing local groups that aimed to influence and bolster GOP political campaigns.

Scholars who study protest movements say the Trump presidency has triggered larger and more frequent demonstrations than have been seen in recent memory. Most notably, the Women's March the day after Trump's inauguration saw more than 4 million people in Washington and elsewhere participate in anti-Trump demonstrations—the largest single-day set of protests in US history. And up to 1.2 million people took part in 950 rallies, marches, sit-ins or other forms of political activity in April, according to academics tracking protests across the United States. Since Trump took office, Washington has seen several marches that drew 50,000 or more participants protesting administration policies on climate change, science and racial justice, among other issues.

While most protests—whether directed at Trump or involving other issues—have been peaceful, some have spawned violence and even death. Last August in Charlottesville, Va., a suspected neo-Nazi drove his car into a crowd of counter-protesters, killing one and injuring 35. Vandalism and violence also have erupted in some protests against police brutality, including the murder of five police officers by a sniper during an otherwise peaceful protest in Dallas in July 2016. In response to violent or disruptive demonstrations, especially those that block highway traffic or other infrastructure, five states have imposed restrictions on protests, and more than a dozen others have considered doing so.

Dana Fisher, a sociologist at the University of Maryland, College Park, who is writing a book about protests in the Trump era, says she is not surprised that the number of protests are up. Protests occur more frequently during Republican administrations, she says, and "we have a man in the White House who seems to be very intent on creating what we [academics] call moral outrage. That has been a boon for protest, for sure."

Most academics who study protests agree that activism tends to be a tactic preferred by the left, citing the civil rights, free-speech and antiwar movements of the 1960s, the anti-nuclear and anti-globalization movements of the 1980s and '90s, and more recently the Occupy Wall Street and Black Lives Matter movements. However, David Meyer, a sociologist at the University of California, Irvine, who studies protests, says conservative, antiabortion activists "have been the most stalwart over the last 40 years, showing up in big demonstrations in Washington, D.C., and [at] site-based protests, including outside clinics, at least since the 1970s."

The rights to assemble and petition the government are enshrined in the Constitution. A 2017 Pew Research Center poll found that 79 percent of Americans believe it is "very" important that people have the right to nonviolent protest, and 74 percent believe it is "very" important that the "rights of people with unpopular views are protected."

However, Meyer says many Americans tend to disapprove of protests that are provocative or turn violent, especially if they disagree with the cause. "We're very uncomfortable when people we disagree with protest," he says. Such protests are seen as "disruptive and costly and unpleasant."

On campuses, some students have tried to block provocative speakers, leading to criticism they are squelching free speech. Racist speakers in particular, such as white nationalist Richard Spencer, have drawn large oppositional and disruptive crowds, some of which have turned violent. And some speakers on the left have drawn protests on a few campuses.

"Unfortunately, what all of us are seeing across the country, more and more, is a threat to that marketplace of ideas, with people trying to shut down others with different perspectives," says John Hardin, director of university relations at the Charles G. Koch Charitable Foundation, a conservative group that promotes open debate on campus.

In recent years, protests organized by the Black Lives Matter movement against police brutality and killings of unarmed African-Americans have involved disruptive tactics such as shutting down traffic on freeways. In proposing penalties for such actions, Minnesota Republican state Rep. Nick Zerwas says, "You have absolutely zero First Amendment protections or right to assemble in the center lane of Interstate 94."

Many NFL players have protested police shootings of unarmed black men by kneeling during the pregame national anthem, which has generated controversy. Trump said the players should be fired and urged fans to boycott NFL games. Some polls showed that many Americans believe the players were disrespectful of national symbols such as the flag and the anthem. "A threat to symbols feels like a threat to collective identity," says John Inazu, a law professor at Washington University in St. Louis who has written a book about freedom of assembly.

But other polls found that Americans supported the players' right to protest, depending on how the questions were phrased, and many found that the public felt Trump's response was inappropriate.

Social media has made it easier to organize protests, regardless of the cause. "Social media is a remarkable tool not only for mobilizing people but also for spreading information about logistics, medicine, transportation and other issues," says Joshua Tucker, co-director of the Social Media and Political Participation lab at New York University. In addition, he notes, after the protests end, social networks can drum up support for other activities, such as raising money for candidates.

As politicians and observers view the current wave of political protests, here are some questions they are debating:

Does Protesting Sway Policymakers?

While the Trump presidency has triggered multiple protests and marches demanding his impeachment, there is little evidence they have led to policy changes at the White House—and they have not forced Trump to leave office.

"If you have a protest of Hillary Clinton voters against Donald Trump, that's not going to be very effective," says Michael Heaney, a political scientist at the University of Michigan. "Many of the protests that we've seen this year have not been super effective."

Some street protests are organized primarily to draw media and public attention to an issue rather than to change policy, says Greg Magarian, a law professor at Washington University. "Street protest is the classic, inexpensive way of getting your message out," he says.

Street protests alone may not be enough to convince policymakers to change course on an issue, however, says Stan Veuger, a resident scholar at the American Enterprise Institute, a conservative think tank. Protests must be followed up with efforts to lobby politicians or engage in direct negotiation with institutional leaders, he says. "I don't think going somewhere and shouting convinces people who are not already convinced of your viewpoint," he says, "but it may help with mobilizing."

Meyer, the University of California sociologist, agrees. "Protest is effective when it takes place in concert with a range of other political activities—when it inspires people to do other things. It's not just the event, it's the context in which it takes place."

But having activists from around the country flood switchboards is not as effective as having constituents call. It is standard practice for congressional staffers to ask for callers' ZIP codes, so they can determine which callers are constituents. However, even constituent protests are not always effective.

For instance, citizens who were worried about Republican efforts to overhaul the Affordable Care Act ("Obamacare") flooded Capitol Hill switchboards last year. "Since last Thursday, the

Cochran offices have received approximately 224 constituent calls against and two in favor of [the] draft of the health care bill," Chris Gallegos, communications director for Mississippi Republican Sen. Thad Cochran, told *Politico* in June. Yet Cochran ended up voting for the legislation.

Conversely, when the act was enacted in 2010, it was done despite protests from the tea party and other skeptics, and poll numbers showing more people disapproved of it than supported it. (Ironically, the law's poll numbers improved in 2017 as congressional action toward repeal became more likely.)

"Protests rarely have outcomes in terms of passing a bill or affecting a presidential policy," says Fisher, the Maryland sociologist. But protests still can help focus attention or bring concerned people together to continue working on an issue, she says.

Persistence is key, says Don Mitchell, an American scholar of protests who teaches at Uppsala University in Sweden. Sometimes the importance of a particular protest as a turning point on an issue is only understood in retrospect, he says. For instance, he says, "the media was really dismissive" of people protesting the House Un-American Activities Committee in San Francisco in 1960. "But then if you look at the histories, people talk about it as a really important moment."

In 2011, when Occupy Wall Street protesters against income inequality began occupying public spaces in New York City and around the country, the movement appeared to be leaderless and lacking in specific demands. It faded quickly from the scene. But it had a lasting impact by highlighting economic disparity as an issue.

"Occupy, which a lot of people see as ineffectual, changed the way we think about income inequality," says Magarian.

Few causes have seen such consistent support from activists as the anti-abortion movement. Since the Supreme Court legalized abortion in 1973, opponents have held annual marches in Washington, employed disruptive tactics such as blocking access to clinics and have coupled street protests with intense lobbying. Although the public remains divided on the issue, dozens of states have enacted hundreds of restrictions on the procedure in recent years.

Given the nature of street protests, dominated by slogans demanding immediate action, it is difficult to persuade some participants to work for a cause over many years, says Meyer. "It's hard to get people to show up and say, 'We're going to march as part of a 60-year process toward racial and economic progress,'" he says. But those who succeed in changing policy "recognize it's a long-haul process, and protest is one piece of that story."

"Movements don't write legislation," said Nina Eliasoph, a sociologist at the University of Southern California. "They force open a line of questions that makes it possible for people to imagine new policies. That's always the first step."

[...]

Challenges to Dissent

The United States was founded in an act of protest—a rebellion against British colonial power. The Revolutionary War was preceded by protests, such as the Boston Tea Party of 1773, a celebrated example of vandalism in defiance of taxes.

The First Amendment to the Constitution enshrined the rights to free speech and freedom of assembly and the right to petition the government. But within a few years, President John Adams convinced Congress to pass the Alien and Sedition Acts, laws enacted in 1798 designed to crack down on immigrants and political enemies.

The Sedition Act barred public opposition to the government, including "any false, scandalous, and malicious writing" against the government of the United States, Congress, or the president, with intent to defame, or "bring either into contempt or disrepute." Rep. Matthew Lyon of Vermont, who was convicted under the act, complained that Adams had "a continual grasp for power" and would turn people out of office if he disagreed with them. The next president, Thomas Jefferson, persuaded Congress to repeal most of the laws and pardoned those still in prison for breaking them.

Some protest movements were hugely influential during the 19th and 20th centuries, including the abolitionist movement against slavery, the temperance movement to ban alcohol and the labor movement's effort to outlaw child labor and other practices. Yet serious protests have often met with resistance from government authorities.

"There was no time in American history when all views could be aired without some restrictions," says Kazin, the Georgetown historian. "There have always been some views that some people thought were so repugnant and dangerous that they couldn't be allowed to be heard."

For instance, after the United States entered World War I in 1917, Congress sought to shut down dissent by enacting the Espionage Act of 1917 and the Sedition Act of 1918, which banned protests against the war or speech or publication "disloyal" to the government, soldiers or the American flag. "It is extremely dangerous to exercise the constitutional right of free speech in a country fighting to make democracy safe in the world," lamented Eugene V. Debs, a socialist labor organizer and presidential candidate, in a 1918 speech for which he was arrested.

The Supreme Court upheld Debs' conviction in 1919, part of a trio of decisions affirming the constitutionality of the wartime acts. One case, *Schenck v. United States*, prompted Justice Oliver Wendell Holmes' famous comment, "The most stringent protection of free speech would not protect a man in falsely shouting fire in a theatre and causing a panic." The court upheld the conviction of Charles Schenck, the Socialist Party secretary, for publishing a pamphlet opposing the military draft. (The court overturned the decision in 1969, in *Brandenburg v. Ohio*, stating that speech is protected unless it is "directed to inciting or producing imminent lawless action and is likely to incite or produce such action.")

After the war, thousands of unemployed veterans occupied parts of Washington, D.C., in 1932, at the height of the Great Depression, demanding early payment of military bonuses. Many citizens saw the veterans, the so-called Bonus Army, as heroes. But the authorities saw them as subversives bent on taking over the government. Gen. Douglas MacArthur used tanks and saber-wielding cavalry to disperse the protesters.

In 1941, in *Cox v. New Hampshire*, the Supreme Court ruled that governments can impose reasonable "time, place and manner" restrictions on when and where protests and demonstrations can be held.

"That makes sense for all sorts of reasons, for keeping the public order," says Heaney, the Michigan political scientist. "You don't want to have protests at 3 a.m., when people are trying to sleep.

"But when states and localities try to regulate protests," he continues, "they often do so with purposes that are not in the public interest. They'll try to use that power to … put [protests] in very inconvenient places where they really can't be heard."

Nonviolent Protests

After the Supreme Court's historic ruling in *Brown v. Board of Education* in 1954 that segregation in public schools is unconstitutional, there was massive resistance in the South to integrating schools or giving blacks voting or other rights. "Southern state legislatures moved quickly to block any efforts toward school desegregation," wrote historians Maurice Isserman of Hamilton College in Clinton, N.Y., and Georgetown's Kazin. During that era, some legislatures added Confederate battle standards to their state flags.

In response, the civil rights movement in the 1960s pursued different strategies—including sit-ins, boycotts and marches—to combat racist laws. The most prominent leader of the movement, the Rev. Martin Luther King Jr., insisted on nonviolent protests, similar to those Indian leader Mahatma Gandhi had used successfully in protesting British colonial rule during the first half of the 20th century.

But Americans did not all embrace the civil rights movement. A 1961 Gallup Poll, for instance, found that 61 percent of Americans disapproved of the Freedom Riders, a biracial group that sought to desegregate public transportation in the South, while only 22 percent approved.

"Things that we recognize as effective later on are almost always extraordinarily unpopular when they're happening," says Meyer, the University of California sociologist.

After a 1963 protest campaign in Birmingham, Ala., that led to African-Americans being fire-hosed by police and bombed by the Ku Klux Klan, President John F. Kennedy called for federal civil rights legislation to end discrimination in public accommodations. "The events in Birmingham and elsewhere have so increased the cries for equality that no city or state or legislative body can prudently choose to ignore them," Kennedy said. Months later Kennedy was assassinated. In 1964 President Lyndon Johnson pushed for passage of the Civil Rights Act as a memorial to the slain Kennedy.

King then began pushing for voting rights legislation. On March 7, 1965, protesters attempted to march from Selma, Ala., to the state capitol in Montgomery. They were met along the way by state troopers, sheriff's deputies and vigilantes who tear-gassed and beat them. "Men, women and children were beaten to the ground with billy clubs, cattle prods and bull whips," Isserman and Kazin wrote. "Some marchers were ridden down by horses."

Televised images of the violence against peaceful protesters in Selma shocked the country. Eight days later, Johnson called on Congress to enact the Voting Rights Act, which he signed into law that August.

The civil rights movement's success using nonviolent protests influenced other campaigns. Some participants in other 1960s movements, such as Mario Savio of the Free Speech Movement at UC Berkeley, had been civil rights workers and borrowed from the movement's techniques and strategies. The Free Speech Movement, in turn, helped establish the template for other student protests of the era, such as campus sit-ins to demand concessions from university administrators and marches against the Vietnam War.

"The research shows nonviolence works better," says Fabio Rojas, a sociologist at Indiana University, Bloomington. "When you become violent, you lose respect."

Confrontational Protests

In August 1968, four months after the assassination of Dr. King and the urban riots that his murder triggered across the country, the situation outside the Democratic National Convention in Chicago was anything but nonviolent. Protesters against the Vietnam War were met by police who deployed tear gas and used clubs to beat not only protesters but also reporters and bystanders.

Although official investigators later criticized the police for their actions, a majority of the public supported the police, and Republican Richard M. Nixon, running on a "law and order" platform, won the presidency that year.

Two years later, after Ohio National Guardsmen opened fire at an antiwar protest at Ohio's Kent State University, killing four unarmed students and wounding nine others, outraged students staged protests at hundreds of campuses around the country. Ten days later, two students were killed and 12 more wounded when police opened fire at a protest at Jackson State University in Mississippi.

Law enforcement agencies eventually learned to negotiate with protest leaders, and subsequent protest movements during the 1970s and '80s were largely peaceful. The protesters and police often would agree in advance about the location and timing of demonstrations.

Beginning in the 1970s, after the Supreme Court's Jan. 22, 1973, ruling in *Roe v. Wade* that Americans have a constitutional right to an abortion, anti-abortion protesters have gathered outside the court in Washington every Jan. 22 for the annual "March for

Life." Often they are met by abortion-rights supporters, but the demonstrations usually are peaceful.

"What's happened is this long process where police and local authorities have worked to make it safer and easier to protest, and make it less disruptive," Meyer says.

College authorities and protest organizers began setting up so-called free speech zones, where protesters could hold rallies and listen to speeches. "You could protest all you want, but you could never protest in the places where you might be most effective," says Uppsala's Mitchell.

Over time, some activists chafed at the restrictions or concluded they could have more impact pursuing confrontational tactics. During the 1980s, for instance, the environmental group Earth First! drove nails into trees in an effort to damage saws and discourage logging.

Later that decade, members of ACT UP, a group seeking faster approval and lower prices for anti-AIDS drugs, chained themselves to a balcony at the New York Stock Exchange and blockaded offices at the Food and Drug Administration. The anti-abortion group Operation Rescue, founded in 1987, borrowed blockading tactics from leftist groups. Separately, at least 11 people have been killed by anti-abortion extremists since 1993.

"Earth First! and the other new direct action movements of the 1980s and '90s differed from … earlier efforts partly in temperament: They were pushier and more cynical," writes journalist and activist L.A. Kauffman.

During the late 1990s and early 2000s, anti-globalization protesters who sought to disrupt World Bank and International Monetary Fund meetings blocked traffic and in some cases vandalized property. During the "battle for Seattle" in 1999, some 50,000 demonstrators were met outside a World Trade Organization (WTO) conference by police and the National Guard. The crowd—one of the earliest mass protests organized via the internet—was larger than expected and helped kick off the anti-globalization movement.

After that confrontation—and the Sept. 11, 2001, terror attacks in the United States two years later—the WTO tightened security at its international meetings and moved them to out-of-the way cities with more restrictive protest policies, such as Doha, Qatar. Protesters were quarantined in fenced-off free speech zones, sometimes far from the site of main events.

"A decade followed of really intense protest fencing, making protests not heard," says Mitchell. "That led to escalation of tactics on the part of dissidents, who feel the only way they can get heard is being more extreme in their tactics."

In 2008, Obama was elected in the midst of a crippling international financial crisis and the 2007-09 recession. His efforts to expand health coverage and rejuvenate the economy through deficit spending prompted the tea party protest movement on the right, which began with rallies that drew tens of thousands of participants around the country on April 15, 2009 (the deadline day for filing federal income tax returns).

In time, the tea party became a loose amalgam of hundreds of local organizations—including 800 with about 200 active members each—allied with well-funded conservative groups such as FreedomWorks and Americans for Prosperity, helping to push Republican candidates further to the right.

The other major populist movement of the Obama presidency was the left-leaning Occupy Wall Street movement, led by people angry about the growing income disparity between the wealthiest 1 percent of the population and the poorest members of society. Members occupying a park near Wall Street in 2011 chanted "we are the 99 percent." The movement quickly spread to more than 100 cities, with protesters staging sit-ins at banks and blocking traffic, leading to roughly 5,500 arrests. But without clear demands or leaders, the movement eventually faded away.

In recent years, many of the nation's most prominent protests have revolved around the issue of police violence. The social media hashtag #BlackLivesMatter first emerged following the 2013 acquittal of George Zimmerman, a member of a neighborhood watch group in Florida who was acquitted after shooting an unarmed black teen, Trayvon Martin.

But the movement took on greater currency a year later when a police officer in Ferguson, Mo., killed an unarmed black teen, Michael Brown. A series of high-profile police killings of black suspects in recent years has led to protests in cities across the country.

In recent years, protesters have sought to block construction of oil pipelines, notably the Dakota Access and Keystone XL projects. Both have seen confrontations between police and protesters who built encampments designed to block the construction. But with both projects gaining final approval during the Trump administration, the protests have dwindled.

[…]

Outlook: Continuing Conflict

Protest, by its nature, involves conflict. With a president who is controversial and unabashedly confrontational, few observers believe the current wave of protests will calm down soon.

"Trump loves the fight—he loves goading people," says McAdam, the Stanford sociologist. "He's picking a fight, and the left is picking up on it."

Political consultants say a lot may depend on how elections this year and in 2020 turn out.

"2018 is what I'm all about," says Taussig, the St. Louis protester.

Trump's opponents on the left threatened in advance to take to the streets if he fires Robert Mueller, the special counsel investigating the Trump campaign's alleged collusion with Russia. Some conservatives, by contrast, have warned that the president's supporters will riot if Trump is impeached. "Try to impeach him. Just try it," Roger Stone, a longtime Trump political adviser, said last August. "You will have a spasm of violence in this country, an insurrection like you've never seen."

In an era when the country is deeply polarized, continuing conflict between the political parties and their supporters appears to be almost a given. Some observers worry that the Charlottesville clash could become an ugly precursor to increased political violence. Scattered acts of violence have occurred in and around politics—such as a liberal opening fire at a Republican congressional baseball practice in June in Alexandria, Va.—and death threats have become routine against some politicians.

"We have become inured to violent speech," says Fisher, the University of Maryland professor. She's hoping for a return to civility and respect, but she fears continued disagreement could devolve into more physical confrontations.

"I worry that the nature of protests, because they're so emotive and often angry, don't facilitate finding the unsexy common ground needed to change policy in the long term," says Inazu, the Washington University law professor.

To make matters worse, Americans' willingness to confront one another in the streets was manipulated by Russians via social media during the 2016 presidential campaign. A Facebook group called on people to attend a noon rally at an Islamic center in Houston on May 21, 2016, to "Stop Islamification of Texas." Another Facebook group called for a "Save Islamic Knowledge" protest at the same time and place. Observers thought it was a protest and a counter-protest.

But it turned out the opposing rallies had both been organized by Facebook groups controlled by Russians who purchased $200 worth of Facebook ads. "From a computer in St. Petersburg, Russia, these operators can create and promote events anywhere in the United States ... to tear apart our society," North Carolina Republican Sen. Richard Burr, who chairs the Senate Intelligence Committee, said at a hearing in November.

Politicians from both parties are calling for a return to civility and less bitterness. "We have seen our discourse degraded by casual cruelty," former President George W. Bush, a Republican, said in October. "Argument turns too easily into animosity. Disagreement escalates into dehumanization."

"All too often, tribalism based on race, religion, sexual identity and place of birth has replaced inclusive nationalism, in which you can be proud of your tribe and still embrace the larger American community," former President Bill Clinton, a Democrat, wrote in a recent op-ed. "From Charleston to Charlottesville, we are reminded that the racial divide remains a curse that can be revived with devastating consequences."

For protests to be an expression of something other than anger or dissatisfaction, movements must have some sort of policy change or other goal in mind.

"Anger is not enough," says Rojas, the Indiana sociologist. "You need concrete plans. That's what matters. The difference between short-term protests and something long-term like women's rights or the pro-life movement is getting away from just being angry, to saying 'this is exactly what I want.' "

[...]

16

Populism and Outrage Around the World

Dean Baker

Dean Baker co-founded the Center for Economic and Policy Research, where he serves as senior economist. He is the author of several books, including Rigged: How Globalization and the Rules of the Modern Economy Were Structured to Make the Rich Richer.

In this excerpted viewpoint, economist Dean Baker asserts that populist movements around the world are not merely the product of mass hysteria, but have an economic basis. While the ways in which a movement's anger manifests—including xenophobia and racism—may not have a logical basis, economics can help account for how these movements begin. Baker looks at populist movements in the United Kingdom, France, Italy, Spain, and the United States to explore the connection between economics and populism, ultimately making the argument that the economic factors at play must be addressed to quell populist outrage.

The growth of populist movements across the world is impossible to ignore at this point. The last decade has seen a huge expansion in support of populism of both the right and left, although populism of the right is generally much stronger.

This populist surge has been behind the decision of the United Kingdom to leave the European Union, parties challenging for power on the right in France and Italy, as well as several smaller

"The Rise of Populism: The Masses Have a Case," by Dean Baker, Center for Economic and Policy Research, March 27, 2017, http://cepr.net/publications/briefings/testimony/the-rise-of-populism-the-masses-have-a-case. Licensed under CC BY 4.0 International.

European countries, and on the left in Spain. Left populists actually managed to gain power in Greece. And of course populist sentiments were a major force in the election of Donald Trump, as there was a massive swing in support among white working class voters towards the Republicans in the last election.

While it is hard to put together a coherent economic agenda from populist platforms, there are some common themes. The populist message, from the both the left and right, is that the typical person is not getting their share of the benefits of economic growth. The left populists generally blame some set of corporate elites, the right generally turns to immigrants and racial and ethnic minorities as their villains. The populists of the right usually promise to put their national group above the foreign elements who are seen as the threat, thereby restoring prosperity to true French people, Italians, Americans or whoever.

While there can be little basis for sympathy for the racism and xenophobia pushed by right-wing populist leaders, there is a real economic basis for the anxiety of the groups to whom they are appealing. We have to take this anxiety seriously, not only because it threatens the future of democracy, but we as economists deserve much of the blame.

In fact, economies in the rich countries have not produced real benefits for much of the population in recent decades. This is certainly true for most rich countries for the last fifteen years, and in the United States, arguably for the last four decades. The failure to deliver growing incomes for the large segments of the population was not the result of natural forces, but rather conscious policy decisions. I will argue that it is important that we steer rich country governments on a different course, both because it is the right thing to do—policies should not be designed to redistribute income upwards—and also to preserve democracy. We cannot expect the bulk of the population to support governments that do not improve their quality of life.

I will make three main points in this discussion. First, I want to outline the extent to which economic policy in rich countries has failed both to produce growth in aggregate and in particular failed to deliver gains to those in the bottom half of the income distribution. The second point is that this failure is linked to the growth of populist forces. The third and most point is that we can devise alternative policies that are both growth enhancing and also will promote greater equality.

Rich Country Economic Policy: Stagnation and Inequality

Both the economic crisis in 2008 and the weak recovery that followed caught the overwhelming majority of economists by surprise. The fact that asset bubbles were driving growth across much of the world was overlooked by almost the whole profession. None of the official forecasts predicted the recession in 2008 and 2009. In fact, most forecasters failed to recognize the recession, and certainly not its severity, until it was well under way. This mistake was compounded by failing to recognize the weakness of the recovery. The conventional view was that there would be a quick bounce back from a severe recession, as had been the case following prior downturns.

[...]

This growth shortfall by itself would provide a real basis for public dissatisfaction with the conduct of economic policy. After all, mistaken policies that needlessly cost a country several percentage points of GDP are a big deal. When these policies lead to double-digit losses in GDP on an ongoing basis, as is true for many wealthy countries, that provides genuine grounds for the public to be unhappy with those designing economic policy.

However there are even more grounds for anger when the weak overall growth performance is accompanied by an upward redistribution of income. This is exactly what we have seen in most wealthy countries. A recent analysis by the OECD (2015) showed that almost all wealthy countries have seen a rise in inequality in the last two decades. In several cases, the growing share of income going to the wealthy actually has been associated with declines in income for those at the middle and bottom of the income distribution.

[...]

In short, recent decades have not been good economic times for most of the people in the rich countries. When large segments of the population are seeing little or no gains from the economy for a substantial period of time, it is not surprising that they would look to throw out the people who they consider responsible. This is especially likely when they see a relatively small group at the top who appear to be doing very well even as the rest of the country does poorly.

The Motivation for Populism: Racism and Xenophobia or Economic Hardship

There has been a major debate in the last year over the extent to which the upsurge in populist sentiment can be attributed to economic factors, as opposed to a resurgence of racist and xenophobic sentiment. The two cannot easily be disentangled, since many people, particularly those who are less knowledgeable about policy, may mix motives in their minds. I don't expect that this argument can be conclusively resolved, but there are a few simple points that can be made.

First, racism and xenophobia are not new in any of the countries which have seen an upsurge in right-wing populism. The burden on those who would see these as the key factors behind the rise of populism, and especially right-wing populism, is to explain why it has suddenly become such a large political force. Immigration of non-white people to Europe is hardly a new phenomenon. The influx of refugees from Syria and other Middle Eastern countries has been somewhat of a flashpoint, but the rise of populism preceded this influx.

The terrorist incidents in France, Belgium, and elsewhere also have fueled racist and xenophobic attitudes, but again such incidents are not unprecedented and cannot be closely tied to the rise of right-wing populism. Perhaps the most deadly single terrorist attack in recent decades occurred in Madrid in 2004, nonetheless right-wing populism is not a major political factor in Spain. While nowhere has been immune from terrorist attacks, countries like Denmark and the Netherlands have seen strong upsurges in right-wing populism with relatively few incidents.

It is possible to point to political causes in these two cases, as the social democratic parties have been proponents of cuts to welfare state benefits, whereas populist parties have been vigorous supporters of maintaining or strengthening welfare state benefits. This is especially notable in Denmark, where the Danish People's Party repeatedly threatened to withdraw support from conservative governments if they made large cuts in health and education funding.

While racism and xenophobia were undoubtedly important factors in the recent Brexit vote, the supporters of Brexit made explicit economic arguments to advance their case. They promised in a national ad campaign that the money saved on the United Kingdom's contribution to the European Union could be used to shore up the national health system (NHS) if the UK left the EU. While this was not true, the net direct savings were trivial and in any case the UK is not facing a hard budget constraint in its national spending (in other words, cutting back funding for the NHS was a political choice, not an economic necessity) , it seems likely that many people believed it. It is also the case that the quality of health care in the UK has been affected by recent budget cuts. Given these facts, it is reasonable to believe that concern over the quality of the health care system was a major factor for many supporters of Brexit, who tended to be older, and therefore more in need of health care, and lower income.

The US case also provides a difficult challenge to those who want to argue that the issue is simply one of resurgent racism or xenophobia. After having elected an African American president twice, we have to believe that large segments of the white population suddenly became more worried about losing control of the country to non-whites. The immigration story is even less plausible as an explanation in the US than Europe, as immigration has actually slowed substantially in the years since the Great Recession.

In addition to being more openly racist and xenophobic than prior Republican candidates, Trump also distinguished himself from them in being explicitly protectionist. He put reversing "bad" trade deals at the center of his economic agenda. He argued that we lost good paying manufacturing jobs to other countries because our trade negotiators were stupid and got outmaneuvered by the negotiators from Mexico, China, and elsewhere. He promised that he would get good trade deals by threatening or actually imposing large tariffs. He told voters that he would bring back the millions of manufacturing jobs that had been lost to trade.

While this promise may be completely unrealistic, it certainly seems plausible that many voters took it seriously. The key to the election was the flipping of the Midwestern industrial states that had lost a huge percentage of their manufacturing jobs due to the rise in the trade deficit in the last two decades. The state of Ohio, which President Obama had won by comfortable margins twice, went to Trump by over eight percentage points. Trump also carried Michigan, Wisconsin, and Pennsylvania, all of which had voted Democratic in every election since 1988.

There is considerable evidence that Trump saw the greatest improvement in performance relative to prior Republicans in areas that have fared worst in the last two decades. For example, a recent study examined the correlation between deaths due to drugs, alcohol, and suicide, and found that the counties with the highest rates were also the ones where Trump most over-performed relative to prior Republican candidates (Monnat 2016). Other analyses produced similar findings correlated counties with rising mortality rates with Trump voters in the Republican primaries (e.g. Guo 2016).

Perhaps the most compelling case against these lines was a paper by David Autor, David Dorn, Gordan Hanson, and Kaveh Majelsi (2017) that built on their prior work analyzing the impact of imports from China on manufacturing and total employment by commuter zone. Their analysis found a strong correlation between the exposure to imports from China and the shift from Democratic to Republican votes in the 2016 presidential election compared with the 2000 presidential election. By their estimates, if the rise in imports from China had been half as large as what the country actually experienced, Clinton would have carried North Carolina, Pennsylvania, Wisconsin, and Michigan, giving her a victory in the Electoral College.

[...]

Different Political Outcomes from Alternative Economic Policies

The prior discussion is only interesting if there is an alternative economic path that would have produced better outcomes for the bottom portion of the income distribution. While it is common to argue that the upward redistribution of the last four decades is part of an inevitable process of globalization and the development of technology, I would argue that it has been the result of economic policy choices. I will discuss five areas in which alternative economic policies could have led to greater equality without slowing overall growth:

1. Macroeconomic policy—governments have been over-concerned about the threat of inflation at the cost of higher unemployment;

2. Intellectual property rights—there has been a notable strengthening of intellectual property rights in a variety of areas, leading to larger incomes for those in a position to benefit from rents in this area;

3. The growth of finance—there has been an explosion in the size of the financial sector relative to the economy as a whole. This sector is the source of some of the highest incomes in the economy;

4. Corporate governance—the rules of corporate governance have allowed CEOs and other top executives to command an ever larger share of output;

5. Protection of high end professionals—doctors and dentists have seen enormous growth in their pay relative to other workers, in part because they are largely protected from foreign and domestic competition.

My discussion of these topics is necessarily brief, but hopefully will be sufficient to outline the basic case. It is also focused on the situation in the United States, both because this is the country which I know best and also because it is the extreme case in terms of the upward redistribution of income.

[...]

Summing Up a Progressive Populist Agenda

It is indisputable that there has been a massive upward redistribution of market incomes in the United States and most other wealthy countries over the last four decades. I have argued that this upward redistribution has been largely due to policy choices, not the natural development of globalization technology. The paper outlines five specific areas in which alternative policies can be put in place to counteract these developments.

While policies in each of these areas can have a substantial impact, the interactive effect is likely to amplify their effect. For example, there are more than 850,000 active physicians in the United States, the vast majority of whom are in the top 2.0 percent of the wage distribution. (The US has roughly 150 million people working in 2017.) If their pay were cut 40 to 50 percent, it would place substantial downward pressure on the pay of the rest of the top 2.0 percent. Similarly, if a financial transactions tax reduced trading volume and revenue by 50 percent (around $100 billion a year) the loss of many extremely high paying jobs would substantially reduce the number of job openings with pay in excess of $1 million a year. In this way, attacking high earners through a variety of mechanisms, as outlined above, can have the same spillover effect on wages at the top end as exposing manufacturing workers to competition from low-paid workers in the developing had on the wages of workers in the middle and bottom.

The broader story is that the market can be structured differently than is now the case in order to generate less inequality. Arguably this can be done in ways that actually increase growth, so there is not tradeoff between growth and inequality. We cannot reasonably expect the public to support economic policies which they do not see as giving them a fair share of the benefits from growth. For this reason, it is essential to look to ways in which the current path can be altered to produce more broadly based gains. The failure to do so is not likely to lead to a political environment that many of us will find very appealing.

It is also worth mentioning that broadly based prosperity in rich countries is likely to be more conducive to growth in developing countries. This is both true in a narrow economic sense and also due to the political environment created. In a narrow economic sense, if rich country GDP is 10 percent lower due to bad macroeconomic policy, this means that rich countries will import substantially less from the developing world. A falloff in imports due to weak economic growth has the same impact as reduced imports due to tariffs or other protectionist measures. It is also worth noting that developing countries share in the benefits of innovation from rich countries, assuming that they are not unnecessarily walled off by restrictive intellectual property rules. This means greater technological dynamism by rich countries will also benefit developing countries.

In terms of the political environment, as president, Donald Trump seems determined to give the world a case study in how right-wing populism can be bad news for the developing world. He has indicated a willingness to arbitrarily alter longstanding trade agreements, with little concern for the impact on our trading partners. His first budget calls for large cuts in foreign aid, including an end to any assistance to the developing world in dealing with climate change. And, he proposes restrictions on immigration that reverse practice in the United States, even if not necessarily changes in the law. This is all being done with little, if any, regard for the impact on the countries from which people are emigrating.

For these reasons developing countries have a clear stake in having rich countries pursuing policies that have economic benefits for the bulk of the population. If we continue on the current course, the outcomes are not likely to be very good.

Organizations to Contact

The editors have compiled the following list of organizations concerned with the issues debated in this book. The descriptions are derived from materials provided by the organizations. All have publications or information available for interested readers. The list was compiled on the date of publication of the present volume; the information provided here may change. Be aware that many organizations take several weeks or longer to respond to inquiries, so allow as much time as possible.

The American Civil Liberties Union (ACLU)
125 Broad St., 18th Floor
New York, NY 10004
phone: (212) 549-2500
website: www.aclu.org

For nearly 100 years, the ACLU has been the nation's guardian of liberty, working in courts, legislatures, and communities to defend and preserve the individual rights and liberties that the Constitution and the laws of the United States guarantee everyone in the country.

Bill of Rights Institute
1310 North Courthouse Rd. #620
Arlington, VA 22201
phone: (703) 894-1776
email: info@billofrightsinstitute.org
website: www.billofrightsinstitute.org

Established in September 1999, the Bill of Rights Institute is a nonprofit educational organization that works to engage, educate, and empower individuals with a passion for the freedom and opportunity that exist in a free society. The Institute develops educational resources and programs for a network of more than 50,000 educators and 70,000 students nationwide.

Constitutional Rights Foundation (CRF)
601 S. Kingsley Dr.
Los Angeles, CA 90005
phone: (213) 487-5590
website: www.crf-usa.org

The Constitutional Rights Foundation is a nonprofit, nonpartisan, community-based organization dedicated to educating America's young people about the importance of civic participation in a democratic society. Under the guidance of a Board of Directors chosen from the worlds of law, business, government, education, the media, and the community, CRF develops, produces, and distributes programs and materials to teachers, students, and public-minded citizens all across the nation.

Convergence Center for Policy Resolution
1133 19th St. NW, Suite 410
Washington, DC 20036
phone: (202) 830-2310
email: info@convergencepolicy.org
website: www.convergencepolicy.org

The Convergence Center for Policy Resolution is a nonprofit organization focused on solving social challenges through collaboration. The Convergence team brings deep knowledge of policy and process and works with leaders and doers to move past divergent views to identify workable solutions to seemingly intractable issues.

First Amendment Center – Vanderbilt University
John Seigenthaler Center
1207 18th Ave. S
Nashville, TN 37212
phone: (615) 727-1600
website: www.firstamendmentcenter.org

The First Amendment Center supports the First Amendment and builds understanding of its core freedoms through education, information, and entertainment. The center serves as a forum for the study and exploration of free-expression issues, including freedom of speech, of the press, and of religion, and the rights to assemble and to petition the government. Founded by John Seigenthaler, the First Amendment Center is an operating program of the Freedom Forum and is associated with the Newseum and the Diversity Institute. The center has offices in the John Seigenthaler Center at Vanderbilt University in Nashville, Tennessee, and at the Newseum in Washington, DC.

National Constitution Center
Independence Mall
525 Arch Street
Philadelphia, PA 19106
phone: (215) 409-6600
website: www.constitutioncenter.org

The National Constitution Center is the first and only institution in America established by Congress to "disseminate information about the United States Constitution on a non-partisan basis in order to increase the awareness and understanding of the Constitution among the American people." The Constitution Center brings the United States Constitution to life by hosting interactive exhibits and constitutional conversations and inspires active citizenship by celebrating the American constitutional tradition.

Pew Research Center
1615 L St. NW, Suite 800
Washington, DC 20003
phone: (202) 419-4300
website: www.pewresearch.org

The Pew Research Center is a nonpartisan fact tank that informs the public about the issues, attitudes, and trends shaping the world. It conducts public opinion polling, demographic research, media content analysis, and other empirical social science research. Pew Research Center does not take policy positions.

PolitiFact
1100 Connecticut Ave. NW, Suite 440
Washington, DC 20036
phone: (202) 463-0571
website: www.politifact.com

PolitiFact is a fact-checking website that rates the accuracy of claims by elected officials and others who speak up in American politics.

Southern Poverty Law Center
400 Washington Ave.
Montgomery, AL 36104
phone: (334) 956-8200
website: www.splcenter.org

The Southern Poverty Law Center monitors hate groups and other extremists throughout the US and exposes their activities to law enforcement agencies, the media, and the public.

Bibliography

Books

Jeffrey M. Berry and Sarah Sobieraj, *The Outrage Industry.* New York, NY: Oxford University Press, 2014.

Manuel Castells, *Networks of Outrage and Hope: Social Movements in the Internet Age.* Cambridge, UK: Polity Press, 2012.

Martin Durham, *White Rage: The Extreme Right and American Politics.* New York, NY: Routledge, 2007.

Gemma Edwards, *Social Movements and Protest (Key Topics in Sociology).* Cambridge, UK: Cambridge University Press, 2014.

Joshua Greene, *Moral Tribes: Emotion, Reason, and the Gap Between Us and Them.* New York, NY: Penguin Books, 2014.

Jonathan Haidt, *The Righteous Mind: Why Good People Are Divided by Politics and Religion.* New York, NY: Vintage Books, 2012.

Greg Jobin-Leeds, *When We Fight, We Win: Twenty-First-Century Social Movements and the Activists That Are Transforming Our World.* New York, NY: The New Press, 2008.

John Kasich, *Two Paths: America Divided or United.* New York, NY: Thomas Dunne Books, 2017.

Greg Lukianoff, *Freedom from Speech.* New York: Encounter Books, 2014.

Thomas E. Mann and Norman J. Ornstein, *It's Even Worse Than It Looks: How the American Constitutional System Collided with the New Politics of Extremism.* Philadelphia, PA: Basic Books, 2012.

David S. Meyer, *The Politics of Protest: Social Movements in America*. New York, NY: Oxford University Press, 2006.

Darren Mulloy, *American Extremism: History, Politics, and the Militia Movement (Routledge Studies in Extremism and Democracy)*. New York, NY: Routledge, 2004.

David Neiwert, *Alt-America: The Rise of the Radical Right in the Age of Trump*. New York, NY: Verso, 2017.

Robert Reich, *Beyond Outrage: What Has Gone Wrong with Our Economy and Our Democracy, and How to Fix It*. New York, NY: Vintage Books, 2012.

Ben Shapiro, *Bullies: How the Left's Culture of Fear and Intimidation Silences Americans*. New York, NY: Simon & Schuster, 2013.

Charles J. Sykes, *How the Right Lost Its Mind*. New York, NY: St. Martin's Press. 2017.

Vegas Tenold, *Everything You Love Will Burn: Inside the Rebirth of White Nationalism in America*. New York, NY: Nation Books, 2018.

Heather Ann Thompson, *Speaking Out: Activism and Protest in the 1960s and 1970s*. New York, NY: Pearson Higher Education, 2009.

Periodicals and Internet Sources

Jeffrey M. Berry and Sarah Sobieraj, "The Roots and Impact of Outrage-Mongering in U.S. Political Opinion Media," Scholars Strategy Network, October 27, 2014. https://scholars.org/brief/roots-and-impact-outrage-mongering-us-political-opinion-media

Peter Beinart, "The Rise of the Violent Left," *Atlantic*, September 2017. https://www.theatlantic.com/magazine/archive/2017/09/the-rise-of-the-violent-left/534192/

Russell Berman, "What's the Answer to Political Polarization in the U.S.?" *Atlantic,* March 8, 2016. https://www.theatlantic.com/politics/archive/2016/03/whats-the-answer-to-political-polarization/470163/

Lorraine Boissoneault, "Eleven Times When Americans Have Marched in Protest in Washington," *Smithsonian Online,* January 17, 2017. https://www.smithsonianmag.com/history/suffrage-civil-rights-war-and-puppets-when-and-why-americans-have-marched-washington-180961809/

Barry Brownstein, "Political Outrage Has Become Our Way of Life. There Is a Cure." Foundation for Economic Education, December 6, 2018. https://fee.org/articles/political-outrage-has-become-our-way-of-life-there-is-a-cure/

Nate Cohn, "Polarization Is Dividing American Society, Not Just Politics," *New York Times,* June 12, 2014. https://www.nytimes.com/2014/06/12/upshot/polarization-is-dividing-american-society-not-just-politics.html

Justin Curtis, "A Fake America: Cultural Fragmentation and Polarization," *Harvard Political Review,* January 15, 2017. http://harvardpolitics.com/online/fake-america-cultural-fragmentation-polarization/

Steven P. Dinkin, "Sports, Protest and Outrage: A Retrospective," *San Diego Tribune,* September 23, 2018. https://www.sandiegouniontribune.com/news/mediate-this/sd-me-mediatethis0923-story.html

David French, "On Extremism, Left and White," *National Review,* May 30, 2017. http://www.nationalreview.com/article/448108/political-extremism-beleaguers-both-left-and-right

Joshua Hersh, "Extremism Experts Are Starting to Worry About the Left," *Vice News,* June 15, 2017. https://news.vice.com/en_ca/article/3kpeb9/extremism-experts-are-starting-to-worry-about-the-left

Ed Kilgore, "In the Trump Era, America Is Racing Toward Peak Polarization," *New York Magazine*, May 31, 2017. http://nymag.com/daily/intelligencer/2017/05/in-the-trump-era-america-is-racing-toward-peak-polarization.html

Casey Michel, "How Liberal Portland Became America's Most Politically Violent City," *Politico*, June 30, 2017. https://www.politico.com/magazine/story/2017/06/30/how-liberal-portland-became-americas-most-politically-violent-city-215322

Andrew Park, "Is Our Political Outrage Addictive?" *Psychology Today*, September 13, 2012. https://www.psychologytoday.com/us/blog/between-church-and-hard-place/201209/is-our-political-outrage-addictive

Jessica Rettig, "The Rise of Political Extremism and the Decline of Decency," *US News*. April 8, 2010. https://www.usnews.com/opinion/articles/2010/04/08/the-rise-of-political-extremism-and-the-decline-of-decency

Andrew Soergel, "Is Social Media to Blame for Political Polarization in America?" *US News*, March 20, 2017. https://www.usnews.com/news/articles/2017-03-20/is-social-media-to-blame-for-political-polarization-in-america

Kenneth T. Walsh, "Polarization Deepens in American Politics," *US News*. October 3, 2017. https://www.usnews.com/news/ken-walshs-washington/articles/2017-10-03/polarization-deepens-in-american-politics

"Political Polarization, 1994-2017," Pew Research Center, October 20, 2017. http://www.people-press.org/interactives/political-polarization-1994-2017/

Index